LP-ROM SPE
The break ... warm flower
print].
Spencer-S

D0253881

SA MAR 2015
Ru June '19

## SPECIAL MESSAGE TO READERS

### THE ULVERSCROFT FOUNDATION
**(registered UK charity number 264873)**

was established in 1972 to provide funds for research, diagnosis and treatment of eye diseases. Examples of major projects funded by the Ulverscroft Foundation are:-

- The Children's Eye Unit at Moorfields Eye Hospital, London
- The Ulverscroft Children's Eye Unit at Great Ormond Street Hospital for Sick Children
- Funding research into eye diseases and treatment at the Department of Ophthalmology, University of Leicester
- The Ulverscroft Vision Research Group, Institute of Child Health
- Twin operating theatres at the Western Ophthalmic Hospital, London
- The Chair of Ophthalmology at the Royal Australian College of Ophthalmologists

You can help further the work of the Foundation by making a donation or leaving a legacy. Every contribution is gratefully received. If you would like to help support the Foundation or require further information, please contact:

**THE ULVERSCROFT FOUNDATION**
**The Green, Bradgate Road, Anstey**
**Leicester LE7 7FU, England**
**Tel: (0116) 236 4325**

**website: www.foundation.ulverscroft.com**

# THE BREAKING WAVE

Harriet owes a debt to Rick Seton's family, and to repay it she gives up her job to help Rick set up the Breaking Waves Surf School in Roslarren. But there are problems — notably the arrival of Jem Williams, intent on finding a suitable venue for his geology courses, for which their building would be suitable. Attracted to Jem, Harriet strives to remain loyal to Rick's interests. Can the two be reconciled and Harriet and Jem find lasting happiness together?

*Books by Sheila Spencer-Smith
in the Linford Romance Library:*

THE PEBBLE BANK
A LOVE SO TRUE

# SHEILA SPENCER-SMITH

◆

# THE BREAKING WAVE

*Complete and Unabridged*

## LINFORD
*Leicester*

First published in Great Britain in 2013

First Linford Edition
published 2014

Copyright © 2013 by Sheila Spencer-Smith
All rights reserved

A catalogue record for this book is available
from the British Library.

ISBN 978–1–4448–2193–2

Published by
F. A. Thorpe (Publishing)
Anstey, Leicestershire

Set by Words & Graphics Ltd.
Anstey, Leicestershire
Printed and bound in Great Britain by
T. J. International Ltd., Padstow, Cornwall

This book is printed on acid-free paper

# 1

Treading carefully, Harriet made her way across the uneven soggy ground towards the Cheesewring on Bodmin Moor. She avoided a pool of dark water and wished she had changed her sandals for more suitable footwear.

Intrigued by the miles of open space, she had decided to leave the busy A30 and drive down narrow high-banked lanes to unfenced ones across the moor. Rattling across a cattle grid, she then had to avoid bedraggled sheep and wandering ponies. There were black cattle too, each with a strip like a wide white ribbon tied round their middles.

Strands of hazy mist shrouded the far horizon now and a few stunted trees bowing away from the prevailing wind lent an air of mystery that felt satisfying. She had plenty of time to linger here as she wasn't expected at Breaking Waves

Surf School, Roslarren until five o'clock this afternoon when the last surfing session of the day was due to finish.

'I'm so glad you're coming, Harriet,' Rick had said on the phone, his voice full of enthusiasm for his latest project. 'It's a great life here in Cornwall. You'll love it.'

Rick's family and her own had met and become friends while holidaying in Switzerland when both she and Rick had been fourteen. When her father had died in a climbing accident two years later and her mother had become ill with worry and exhaustion, the Seton family had been wonderfully supportive and generous. She was glad, now, to have the opportunity to repay a little of that kindness when Rick's father, frail now and old beyond his years, had voiced his deep concern for his son's plans.

'A surf school?' Harriet had said with interest when Rick told her of the large house, once a hotel, somewhere near Newquay on the north coast of Cornwall he had inherited. 'That sounds ambitious.'

'I've been down there to have a good look at the area and to do a bit of research. It seems a live-in surfing school would be popular. The owner of the surf shop in town likes the idea and she'll advertise it for us.'

The house needed work but not much. His great aunt had left the bedrooms as they were and lived mainly downstairs for the short time she had occupied the place. There was plenty of storage for surfboards and a huge drying room. Hearing about it, Harriet had felt a growing spark of excitement too because Rick was so obviously delighted with the idea.

'Why don't you join me, Harriet?' he had said.

'Me?'

'I need someone to oversee the running of the place while I concentrate on teaching. You're great with accounts and that sort of thing. You'll be able to learn to surf too. I know you like a challenge.'

And she did. But her job prospects were about to take an upturn. The manager of the restaurant where she worked had decided to take early retirement and as deputy manager she was next in line for the post. It was what she had always wanted and it had taken many sleepless nights to be sure she was making the right decision in turning it down.

'You're crazy, Harriet,' her closest friend at work had said. 'You won't get a chance like this again.'

She had smiled, quite certain by this time that helping Derek Seton's son was the right thing for her to do.

Rick had forgotten about her chance of promotion, but his father hadn't, when she tentatively suggested to him that she should join his son in Cornwall instead. By that time she was aware that Derek Seton's desperate worry was making him ill. It had taken a while to convince him she was serious, and now all the legal business was completed and Rick ready and eager to start up

4

the surf school he had long been planning. And soon she would be there too, helping Breaking Waves to be the success he dreamed of.

Thinking she was alone, the hum of voices took Harriet by surprise. She hesitated and for a moment seemed poised between one life and the next. Then she stumbled and, unable to regain her balance, tripped and fell into one of the peaty pools she had taken pains to avoid.

She was aware of the earthy smell as the splash echoed in her head. Then she felt herself lifted up. She staggered to her feet, blinded by dripping muddy water.

'What have we here?' an amused voice said.

She wiped her eyes, shivering, but was held so firmly she had no choice but to stand there in the grip of a tall stranger clad in hiking gear and with binoculars slung round his neck.

'No, no, I . . . ' she began.

'Just get your breath back,' he said.

'Here, sit down on this hump for a moment.'

There were other offers of assistance, people producing tissues to wipe ineffectually at her clothes — and all wearing sensible hiking boots, she noticed. She took a deep, embarrassed breath and attempted to rub away the mud she suspected covered her face.

The man was smiling down at her and she saw that there were laughter lines deepening the skin round his mouth.

'I'm all right, really,' she said, humiliated. 'Thank you.'

'But you've hurt yourself . . . ' someone began.

'No, no. Really not. Please, I must go. My car's back there.'

But they wouldn't hear of it. Her rescuer stood to one side, half-smiling, as one of the women produced a flask. Before Harriet could prevent it she poured steaming liquid into a cup and handed it to her. Steam rose in the damp air and Harriet tried to drink

6

the coffee scalding hot, spluttering a little and spilling the rest. Mortified, she handed the cup back and struggled to her feet, muttering her thanks.

'Some more?'

'No, no, thanks. I must go.'

'If you're sure . . . '

'Yes, I'm sure.' She felt embarrassed enough by the whole episode without lingering any longer.

There were more murmurs of concern behind her as she left them, sliding a little in her muddy sandals but determined to stay upright. She hoped they had moved off now but wouldn't look back. She hadn't come over the humpy ground very far after all. No other vehicle was parked where she had left her car and she was thankful that she was alone.

The pool nearby was deep and clear and she dipped her muddy hands in and swirled them about. In her bag she had a beach towel and she dampened part of it to scrub her face. Then she towelled her wet hair before having a quick icy paddle. From her suitcase she pulled out a clean jersey and jeans and found her trainers. Her face felt raw from the hard scrubbing she had given it and she felt a lump on her forehead that hadn't been there before. Then she bundled her outer clothes, sandals and towel into a plastic bag and stuffed it deep into the boot of the car.

On her way again she was aware of stiffness in her left arm and her ankle throbbing from twisting it when she fell. She hoped she had given a good impression of nothing much being the matter, that she was used to this sort of thing and thought nothing of it. And in fact it wasn't really an earth-shattering event after all. She was unlikely to see any of them again, even though she couldn't help remembering the sardonic expression on her rescuer's face as she struggled free from his grasp.

Her car was eating up the miles between them now and she would think of him no longer. Soon she saw a thin line of blue on the horizon ahead and knew she was nearly there.

She found the place easily. With the gleaming sea on her left she drove down a steep hill, past a cluster of cottages that was the village of Roslarren, and then up again on the other side. Immediately she saw the large building she recognised from Rick's description as Roslarren House with its sloping lawns in front. A gleaming sign on the wall told her that she had come to the right place, Breaking Waves Surf School. A good situation with wide views of sea and sand, she thought as she drove through the open gates. Perfect.

Several vehicles were parked on the drive, but there was no sign of anyone about and the front door of the house was shut. She got out of her car stiffly and stretched. It was several degrees warmer here than back there on the moor and she could see families scattered about on the sand enjoying themselves. In the surf a crowd of wetsuited figures looked like black seals as they propelled themselves about on their boards. One or two had managed to stand upright and several were surging in on a high wave that broke in a shower of foam as it reached the sand.

It seemed that Rick was still down on the beach. To make sure, she tried the door and found it locked. For a moment she stood and watched with the sun warm on her face. She tried to pick him out among all the activity but failed because at this distance they all looked alike.

Then, behind her, she heard the door creak open.

# 2

The girl who came out to greet her smiled in an engaging way that illuminated her pale face. She pushed strands of light brown hair behind her ears, not seeming to notice that they immediately sprang back.

'You must be Harriet, yes?' she said in a husky voice. 'I'm Dawna Williams, here to greet you. Welcome to Breaking Waves, Harriet. Rick's still down on the beach, as you might have guessed.' She was wearing shorts and a yellow T-shirt with the words 'Breaking Waves' in black letters on the front.

Harriet smiled too. 'I can see I've come to the right place.'

'You'll be wearing one of these too before you've been here five minutes. No, sorry, correction: five hours. Rick's oblivious to time when he gets in the water, and the surf's good today. Let's get your stuff indoors, shall we?'

Harriet lifted out her suitcase and a couple of bags but left her stash of muddy gear where it was. Time enough to deal with that later.

'So,' Dawna said as they went into the house. 'You've known Rick a long time?'

'Since we were teenagers. At least fourteen years.'

'And now you'll be working together?'

'It's a beautiful place.'

'Dawna looked pleased. I love it,' she said. 'I've lived in Roslarren all my life. We're so lucky.'

'I know Rick thinks so,' Harriet agreed.

Dawna smiled. 'I got to know Rick when he came down on visits to his great aunt this last year or two. And now he's inherited this place. The alterations aren't finished yet but you'll know that.'

'Rick warned me.'

'He had the chance to book a group in at once and he took it. That's why we're still in a bit of a mess.'

The bare wooden floors resounded under their feet as they crossed the hall and clattered up the uncarpeted stairs.

'There are a lot of bedrooms,' Dawna said. 'Some larger than others.' She put down the bags she was carrying and leaning against the first door, pushed it open. 'Perfect for when the place is heaving. You've got a whole room to yourself at the moment.'

'And you?'

'I live in a flat over the shop,' said Dawna. 'Not far away. About ten minutes' walk.' She yawned. 'Sorry. A long day. I'm glad you've come to help out, Harriet. Now I'll be able to step back and enjoy a bit of surfing myself in my free time.'

'So you're a keen surfer too?'

Dawna smiled. 'I have to be. Did Rick tell you I'm the owner of the surf shop?'

'Silly question,' said Harriet, smiling too.

'I got the bug years ago in spite of my cousin trying to interest me in rock formations.' She laughed. 'Rocks, can

13

you believe it? But Jem's always been fascinated by stones. Give me surf any day. Can you imagine me striding about looking at cliffs and boulders and suchlike? I haven't got the figure for it like you, Harriet. Short and dumpy, that's me, and proud of it.'

Harriet laughed too. She wasn't dumpy at all. She wouldn't have been able to leap about on a surfboard if she had been.

'Jem's giving a talk at the Olympic Hotel this evening: 'Geoconservation and the Environment'.' Dawna wrinkled her nose. 'That's where I'm off to now, to support him, but I've got to go and change first. He's a great guy really, in spite of wanting to get his hands on this place when the old lady died.' She brightened. 'But surfing's the important thing and Roslarren needs its own surf school. I'm all for it. So what would you like to do first, Harriet?'

'Shower,' said Harriet promptly.

Later, under the jet of steaming water, Harriet thought of the warm welcome Dawna had given her. Before she left she had explained that since there were no vegetarians among them, a large slow cooker was doing duty in the kitchen ready to provide lamb casserole for the evening meal. There was plenty of ice-cream in the freezer for afterwards as well a good supply of fresh fruit and cheese and biscuits. She had stocked up the store cupboard and filled the fridge.

'You won't starve,' she had said with her hand on the door handle. 'And I've laid the table in the dining room for tonight. Sorry I've got to rush, Harriet. See you tomorrow.'

Harriet hadn't wanted to detain her and so hadn't asked how many people there were staying in the house. She would soon find out. Meanwhile she would get herself sorted out and ready to greet Rick and the others when they came up from the beach. A flicker of anticipation filled her as she turned off the water and reached for the clean towel on the rail.

She had time to check the utility room for a washing machine. In here, too, were drying-rails draped with T-shirts and jeans and three thick jerseys. Nearby was a stand for hanging wetsuits, five of them there at the moment. She wondered if one of them was for her, but didn't stop to look closely at them because she wanted to get the contents of her bag of muddy clothes into the machine while she had the chance.

That done, she investigated further. The dining room was another large room at the front of the house, uncarpeted and bare of all furniture apart from a large chest of drawers and a long wooden table with an assortment of dining chairs. Seven sets of cutlery were placed at intervals at one end.

They came soon afterwards, clattering and shouting to one another as they left their surfboards in the spacious room provided. Rick's face lit up on seeing her. He looked glowing as he rushed into the kitchen to give her a hug before he showered and changed.

'Harriet! It's great to see you.'

Laughing, she extricated herself from his rubbery grip. 'As exuberant as ever, Rick.'

'Yep. What do you think of the place? Great, isn't it? You'll love it here. Mmn, something smells good. We're all starving.' His enthusiasm seemed to fill the place. 'There's a lot to tell you,' he said. 'Dawna's been looking after you? So where is she?'

Harriet was surprised. 'Didn't she tell you? She had a previous engagement.'

'That's not like her.'

'She explained everything and she knows I'm more than happy to take over at once. That's what I'm here for, after all.'

'Yep, so you are,' he said. 'I'd better get changed or I'll be holding things up.'

He went off and while he was gone she opened the back door into a yard bordered by outbuildings. One of them was locked but in another she found a chest freezer stocked with more supplies of bacon, sausages, chops and much more. Dawna had done a good job here too.

She was back indoors again by the time everyone else crowded into the kitchen to check what was on the menu for tonight. 'Who's going to carry in the casserole and plates?' Harriet asked.

'Into the other room?' one of the boys asked.

'Come on, Chloë,' said another one. 'Get moving.'

A short girl in a pale pink T-shirt grabbed a tea towel and picked up the plates that Harriet had placed ready. Rick appeared as they seated themselves at the table and slipped into the seat beside Harriet. He looked surprised.

'What's this then?' he said. 'Dining in style tonight, are we?'

Chloë giggled. 'Looks like the kitchen's not good enough.'

'We usually eat in there,' said Rick.

For a moment Harriet was at a loss. Then she smiled. 'I'm celebrating my first day here at Breaking Waves,' she said firmly. 'So the dining room it is tonight. Now who's going to help themselves?'

They were all hungry and set to at once. The younger of the boys put down his knife and fork and reached for the water jug. 'This meat's salty. Pass that jug over here, Neil.'

'Sure will.'

The water jug was empty again and Harriet glanced at the half-empty plates that had been pushed to one side. She got up. 'Shall I make tea now?'

'Yep, good idea,' Rick said. He followed her into the kitchen.

'Could you get the cheese and biscuits in, Rick?' she said. 'And the bread and the fruit. I'll bring the cartons of ice-cream in when I've made the tea. It seems most of them are still hungry.' While waiting for the kettle to boil she found the dishes they needed and put them on a tray with the milk jug and sugar basin.

They ate the rest of the meal in silence. Afterwards while the boys loaded the dishwasher the girls cleared the table and tidied up. The TV was on in the lounge, although some of them looked so exhausted after their first day here that they decided to head for bed.

Rick took Harriet to one side to explain the procedure for next day. 'Low tide at seven a.m.,' he said. 'The sooner we get down there the better, so an early breakfast for those who want it. The first surfing session at nine. You'll be able to make that?'

'I'll be there,' she promised.

'There's a surfboard for you to try out, and a wetsuit. I'll show you tomorrow.' His bright enthusiasm seemed to have faded now and there were deep shadows under his eyes. He yawned. 'It's been a long day.'

She had wanted to ask him about the financial side of things, since she was to be responsible for them, but now was not the time. Early days yet, she reminded herself, and a steep learning curve ahead.

# 3

The bedroom allocated to Harriet was above the dining room. Yesterday she hadn't had much time to marvel at the wide expanse of sea glistening in the sunlight or the distant headlands she could see from her window. Now, waking early, she pulled the flimsy curtains aside. The sun wasn't up properly yet, hardly above the horizon behind the house because a pearly haze hung over land and sea, and the silence was profound. Last night she had been conscious of the continuous surge of the sea but there was nothing now, not even the cry of a distant sea bird.

She shivered, wide awake even though she'd had a disturbed night. She had lain on her hard mattress in the darkness listening to the sea, but seeing in her mind the picture of the granite tor called the Cheesewring on the tourist information board on Bodmin Moor. She had been instantly intrigued by the massive boulders, one on top of the other, outlined against a magnificent blue sky. But her attempt to see it for herself had ended in dismal failure: grey lowering sky instead of blue, no sign of the Cheesewring because she'd ended up in a muddy pool instead, and then being hauled up covered in sludge. She smelt again the peaty earth, and felt the grip of the man's hands and the amusement rippling through him.

The light was strengthening now. A gaggle of seagulls landed on the grass in front of the house and then flew off again, screaming. Time to make a move, early as it was.

Downstairs in the kitchen someone had boiled the kettle and taken the milk out of the fridge. She heard the sound of a door opening and shutting, and then the kitchen door burst open and Mark appeared in a red and black wetsuit. He looked surprised to see her.

'Hi there, Harriet. You're up early.'

'You too. Going somewhere?' She reached the jar of instant coffee from the shelf and spooned some into one of the mugs on the worktop.

'So I'm keen, that's all,' he said. 'Rick says surfing's new to you too. Do you think you'll like it?'

'I think so, if it's not too hard to learn. Rick says I'll pick it up in no time.'

'Don't you believe it,' Mark said with fervour. 'Yesterday we practised getting up on our boards. Rick made us do it for ages and that's before we even got in the sea. You have to do it a certain way and it has to come like second nature. It seemed okay until we got in the water.'

'Then what happened?'

He grinned. 'Guess.'

'You all got up on your feet and were away?'

'So, that shows you've never done it before.' He hooked a stool away from the wall and sat down.

Harriet poured boiling water into her mug and added milk. 'Would you like another hot drink, Mark?'

'Sure. I haven't had one yet. But yes, please — coffee, since you ask. Milk, no sugar.'

'Then who . . . ?'

'Rick I expect. He went out about ten minutes ago. I heard his car start up.'

'He said he was going to get going early today.'

'We were later yesterday. The girls overslept. We had breakfast in here, just helping ourselves as and when. I'll start getting some things on the table, shall I?'

By the time Rick came in bearing a bag of warm croissants, the others had appeared too. Harriet's hope that she and Rick would have some time together to get some arrangements sorted out and to discover exactly what was expected of her were foiled again. All he could think of now was getting them all kitted out and down on the beach by nine o'clock.

The faint mist had cleared, leaving behind the promise of a glorious day.

The sea was a silver sheet and only a ripple disturbed the edge of the sand. The air was salty-fresh and with the tide far out, the low sun cast shadows among the ridges in the hard sand in the distance.

'The surf should get up a bit later,' Rick said with confidence.

Harriet sat with the others on their surfboards in a semicircle and listened as Rick reminded everyone of what they had already learned. He stressed the importance of attaching the leash from their board to their ankles and keeping out of each other's way in the water.

'That's the cord, Harriet,' the girl called Anna murmured.

Rick threw her a look of approval. 'Ten minutes' practice first on dry land,' he said.

They sprang up with enthusiasm. Harriet watched carefully as they did as he said. She tried hard to copy them but somehow her arms and legs wouldn't co-operate. Rick, laughing, came to show her and she tried again.

She was laughing too as she did her best, but it wasn't funny. She could see that everyone was impatient to get in the water.

'Never mind me,' she said. 'I'll practise on my own.'

'I'll be back with you in a minute,' he said.

The others were soon waist-deep demonstrating their prowess. Some got upright straight away and balanced for a few seconds before plunging off with a splash. Others had a great deal of difficulty. Mark, concentrating hard, managed it at last, swayed, and then sank on his board. The wind had got up now and was coming in from the sea. While it had looked calm before, there were now high waves churning up the water into seething white foam.

Harriet watched for a moment and then tried to do as Rick had demonstrated. After a while, with aching limbs, she made a passable show of knowing what she was doing, but she found it hard.

Rick came to join her. 'It's called a pop-up,' he said, watching her. 'There are two ways of doing it: on to your knees and then to your feet, like you're doing, or springing up onto your feet right away.'

She shuddered. 'I'll never master that one.'

'Wait and see. Ready to have a go in the sea now?' he said. 'It's a bit of practice to get the feel of the board, but the waves are breaking all over the place and it's not good. We need good clean ones rolling in to get a good run and not this messy stuff. With luck we'll get it soon.'

The wind wasn't good either, Harriet thought, but the others seemed happy enough. She paddled out to join them. She couldn't believe how hard it was just balancing her weight on the board before she even tried to stand up. Then when she did, her board slid beneath the water and landed up on the bottom.

Mark gave a shout of laughter. 'Fun, isn't it?'

She made a face at him. 'If you say so.' She hauled be board up with difficulty tried again. This time she was too far back and slid off.

Time passed. Rick had them all lying face-down on the boards using their arms to propel themselves along. Then some of them tried to get up on their boards again. Chloë was definitely the best. She was upright for the longest before her board nose-dived for the seabed, and Harriet had the impression that had a suitable wave appeared behind her she would have known instinctively how to use it to her advantage, no problem.

Rick seemed to think so too, because he stayed by her side, encouraging and proud.

'Pasties for lunch,' he called at last. 'Someone needs to fetch them. The order's ready to be picked up. Could you do it, Harriet?'

She was glad of the excuse to be on dry land. 'Of course. Where . . . ?'

'I'll come with you,' said Anna. 'I

know where to go. We got them yesterday.'

'Lead on,' said Harriet.

'Chloë's good, isn't she?' Anna said rather enviously as she and Harriet set off across the sand.

'Better than me, certainly.'

'But you've only just started.'

'Even so.'

'Give yourself a chance, Harriet.'

She didn't think that would make much difference.

'We watched a video on Rick's laptop soon after we got here yesterday,' Anna said. ''Learning to Surf', it was called. It was good. It helped a bit because we all knew in theory what to do even though we found it hard to do in practice.'

'It's early days yet, I suppose, and I'll have plenty of them. There's the whole season ahead. How about you, Anna? How long are you here for?'

'A week, that's all. But we may come back in the summer if we like it. Maybe get holiday jobs down here if we're lucky, because we'll be paying full price then. I'm in my first year at university. Mark is, too, but he's at Exeter and I'm at Durham. He's my brother.'

Harriet would never have guessed. The outgoing Mark towered above his sister, who was quiet and withdrawn. Anna smiled at Harriet's surprise.

The pasty shop was close by and their order was ready for them. They carried them, steamy hot through the paper wrapping, back in companionable silence. Rick had organised the buying of drinks from the kiosk near the beach for today. At other times they'd bring their own down from the house.

After they had eaten, Rick produced tins of wax. 'The boards don't need waxing every time,' he said. 'But you need to know the procedure for when you progress from the learner ones.'

Chloë sat up reluctantly. 'But why?'

'Doing it helps preserve the boards?' Anna suggested.

'That too. But also to give a smoother passage through the water.'

'Makes sense,' said Neil.

The day wore on and there was no change in the state of the surf. Chloë threw herself down on the sand again, a picture of despondency. Harriet could see that everyone felt edgy. They had paddled themselves about until their arms felt sore and floated on their boards, staring up at the sky. The eldest of them, Steven, had almost as much difficulty getting to his feet as Harriet, but practised resolutely long after the others had given up.

Rick glanced at Harriet and shrugged. 'This is hopeless,' he muttered.

She tried to be reassuring. 'What's the forecast for tomorrow?'

'I'll check when we get back.'

She sat with her hands round her knees and looked out to sea. Now that he was a qualified instructor, surfing was all Rick could think of, but there were other ways of enjoying themselves. Lounging here sunk in gloom was no help in the circumstances. She wondered what was in the locked outhouse. A supply of beach equipment?

'Have you got things for beach games?' she asked. 'Footballs, baseball bats, a volleyball net?'

'I hadn't got round to thinking that far ahead,' Rick confessed.

Harriet frowned. Conditions wouldn't always be right for riding the waves, and they weren't today. She could almost feel the boredom coming from them all. Neil picked up a handful of dry sand and ran it slowly through his fingers.

'Who's for a swim?' said Mark suddenly.

No one moved.

'A barbecue?' said Chloë. 'Down here on the beach now the wind's dropping?'

'Yep, that's an idea,' said Rick, his dejection vanishing instantly. 'We've got a brand-new one up at the house, and plenty of charcoal.'

Harriet's mind immediately ran to the packets of sausages she had seen in the freezer. There were chops too, and bacon, and some of those huge beef tomatoes, and large field mushrooms that would do well on a barbecue. Full marks to Dawna for being prepared. 'I'll get myself up there now and start getting things organised,' she said.

'Have you all had enough here?' said Rick.

'Too lazy to move,' said Chloë.

Rick was looking happier now, and the others more alert. Harriet glanced back as she reached the house and saw that one of them was having another go in the water, attempting to remain upright on a board. Hope against experience, she thought.

★  ★  ★

Harriet couldn't believe how much equipment needed to be carried down to the beach. The organisation required kept everyone busy after their showers and the washing-down of their wet-suits. They hung them to dry out in the yard on one of the two washing lines Rick produced from the locked building. He put the other with kit for the beach. 'Might be useful for something,' he said.

Dawna arrived while Harriet was packing the provisions from the fridge into cool boxes. 'Want a hand?'

Harriet stretched. 'I'm beginning to wonder if it's worth all the effort.'

'Sorry I couldn't get here sooner. I had to wait till closing time at the shop. How goes it?'

'Apart from no surf today?'

'Apart from that, of course.'

'A barbecue's on the programme for this evening. Chloë's idea.'

Dawna laughed. 'I like a good barbecue, and the evening's perfect for it.'

They worked together until all the food and drink needed was packed and ready. By then Steven had produced a set of boules and couple of beach balls from the boot of his car. 'Family outings,' he said when someone asked what they were doing in there.

'All set then?' said Rick at last.

Heavily laden, they set off down the slope to the beach and had hardly started when a vehicle drew up behind them.

Dawna spun round. 'Jem!'

'I'm glad I caught you.'

'Only just.'

'I need to ask you something, Dawna. I thought I'd catch you at the shop. Can you spare a minute?'

'Does it look like it?'

'I'll park somewhere and come and find you.'

Some of the others had paused and looked round too, Harriet among them. Then, to her dismay, she realised who Jem was. She felt cold suddenly, as if the evening sun had found a dark, threatening cloud.

Dawna smiled at her as if nothing were the matter. 'My cousin's full of surprises.'

Harriet agreed silently. To meet him again was the last thing she expected, and certainly not here.

'I don't suppose Rick will object if I invite Jem to stay for the evening, do you?' said Dawna.

# 4

By the time they had all made their way onto the beach and decided on a suitable spot to pitch camp, Jem was back with them.

Dawna dropped her load of groundsheets onto the sand and turned to Rick, smiling. 'Rick, this is Jem, who's turned up out of the blue. He's handy with the spatula. D'you mind if he joins us?'

'Ah yes, Cousin Jem,' said Rick. 'Good to see you, Jem. You're welcome.'

Dawna looked round. 'Harriet?'

Harriet had moved away and was busy positioning the cool boxes within easy reach of the barbecue. She still felt hot with embarrassment when she remembered being hauled up out of that muddy pool and Jem's amusement at her predicament. It was a cruel twist of fate that he should be Dawna's cousin and turn up here at this particular time. But with luck he wouldn't recognise her as the clumsy idiot who had landed so ignominiously at his feet. Perhaps she could relax after all.

She risked a glance at him and saw that he was engrossed in doing what was needed with spreading out the groundsheets. Feeling more cheerful now, Harriet helped Dawna arrange their belongings. While Jem got the barbecue going with Chloë's help, the others set up a makeshift volleyball area using the spare washing line that Jem had found.

Harriet sat back on her heels and opened the first cool box, aware of Jem only yards away fixing one end of the rope to a long thin piece of driftwood. She took another look at him and then looked hurriedly away. He appeared to be concentrating fully on the job at hand, but she couldn't help thinking that the little twitch at one side of his mouth might mean that he knew full well who she was.

'All set?' said Dawna at last. 'There's enough food here to feed an army. I hope you feel hungry, folks. All that activity today should have seen to that, yes?'

Harriet smiled at her. 'You're joking, of course?'

'All in day's work. Some good, some bad. But I don't think Rick quite realises that yet.'

Harriet thought of the messy sea causing Rick's despondency and the way it was beginning to affect the others too. 'Not good,' she said.

'As a qualified instructor he should know that. He should have alternative activities on offer.'

Harriet was surprised at the sadness in Dawna's voice. 'Rick said you've given him a lot of help in getting started,' she said.

'I've enjoyed it. Surfing's my life too and I'm glad there's somewhere in Roslarren like Breaking Waves. We needed it. And of course it's good for my business. I supply the wetsuits for a start.'

'But?'

Dawna shrugged. 'There's more than wetsuits in learning to surf. Some are naturals and take to it immediately. Some don't. But all of them should be happy about learning and the atmosphere should be optimistic at all times.'

'D'you think the surf will be better tomorrow?'

'If the forecast is right. Conditions can change quite suddenly here and we don't often have a bad day like today.'

Harriet looked across at the volleyball game, marvelling at the energy of them all. She felt tired just watching. 'I feel pretty sore today. My legs and arms ache as if I'd never used them before. You're not tempted to join in with them, Dawna?'

'I want to get cooking.'

'There won't be much chance of getting near the barbecue if Chloë has anything to do with it.'

Dawna looked across at Chloë and frowned. 'Why can't she play volleyball like everyone else?'

'Where's that food then?' Rick called across to them. They scrambled to their feet.

Soon a mouth-watering smell floated across the beach. After a while the volleyball was abandoned and everyone crowded round, filling plates. Harriet cut hunks of bread, and there was butter and a bowl of salad. Dawna placed the basket of fruit and the box of doughnuts close by.

They sat in a circle to eat. Around them the evening light began to soften. The tide was well in now and tiny waves teased the edge of the sand.

'It's beautiful,' said Harriet dreamily. There was a magic feel in the air now and she wanted this moment to go on forever. Even Jem's presence couldn't spoil it for her and she smiled across at Rick. He was leaning back on one arm watching the members of the group as they cleared their plates.

'That sure is the best meal I've had for ages,' Mark said.

'You always say that,' said Anna.

'This time I mean it.'

Rick's eyes shone and there was a glow of satisfaction about him. 'This is the life. We'll have one every night if you want.'

'But not if it's raining,' said Dawna.

He grinned across at her. 'Ever the pessimistic one,' he said.

'But practical,' said Harriet.

'Have another doughnut,' said Chloë, handing the plate to Mark.

'Sure. Thanks.' He took one and ate it quickly. Then he lay down with his hands behind his head. 'Don't ask me to move,' he said.

'Or me,' said Neil.

'Wake me up when it's time to go,' said Steven.

Jem was eyeing up the cliffs behind them, looking thoughtful. His gaze was so intense that Harriet began to think he expected them to catch fire from the setting sun. Any minute now, sparkling colours would shoot out from them, enveloping them all in glorious Technicolor.

'What's so funny, Harriet?' Rick asked.

She was immediately serious. 'Nothing much. The sun is catching them in just one place.'

Jem turned to her. 'You see it too? The fault line that runs part of the way down? Interesting. I'd like a closer look.'

Dawna smiled at him. 'It's about as interesting as a wet fish.'

'You look as if you want some action, Jem,' said Rick. 'You two girls have done enough work for now. Yep, feel free to wander off if you feel like it. This lot won't be moving for hours.'

Jem quirked an eyebrow at Dawna and Harriet. 'I'd like to take a look further along. Coming?'

'Not me,' said Dawna, unmoving.

Harriet, already on her feet, hesitated. 'Right then,' said Jem, smiling at her. 'Just you and me.'

There was nothing for it but to go with him. He seemed not to notice her discomfort as they walked together away from the others. They were heading for the cliffs further along towards the part that jutted out to form a headland.

He talked of his work that he found so absorbing, and she tried to take in some of the technical terms that made it sound as if he were speaking another language. Seeing her expression, he laughed. 'Sorry. I get carried away sometimes. I forget that the information should be accessible to everyone.'

'Why does it need to be, if they're not interested?'

He stopped still in surprise. 'No one's asked me that before.'

'Sorry. That's a stupid question.'

'Not at all. In fact it's quite a deep one.'

'So what's the answer?'

He was silent for a moment as they started walking again. 'People don't realise just how rich our geological heritage is here in Cornwall,' he said at last. 'If they did, they would understand the importance of conserving it. That's why one of our aims is to raise awareness.'

'Yes, I see that.'

'In the nineteenth century there was a huge protest when the quarry nearby threatened to engulf the Cheesewring. I'm glad to say there's now a restricted area around it. That was the result of local awareness.'

'That would have been terrible.'

'Destroying something that had stood there for millions of years hidden in the surrounding rock that gradually eroded away over time from when the first humans lived on earth. But now it could stand for another million.'

Harriet was silent now as she thought of the implications. He was clearly passionate about these things and wanted others to be enthusiastic too.

'You can see the fleur-de-lis symbol cut into the granite and painted white,' he said. 'If you go there, of course.'

Harriet's cheeks felt warm. 'I see.'

'But you didn't yesterday, did you, up on Bodmin Moor? You didn't get as far as the Cheesewring?'

'Not quite.'

'Another time perhaps.' He made it

sound as if landing flat on your face in a muddy pool was a normal thing to do, but her mouth felt dry when she thought about it.

She cleared her throat. 'So how do you set about making people aware?' she asked.

'We have links with organisations like the National Trust and others who are naturally involved with the environment. We provide guided walks and talks throughout the year.'

'Like yesterday?'

'There's plenty to see up there on Bodmin Moor. Did you know that it's been used by people for the last six thousand years? But tomorrow I'm heading off to Trebarwith Strand near Tintagel. The cliffs there are especially interesting.'

'But they're not in danger of destruction, are they?'

He smiled. 'Not in the next day or two.'

They had reached the end of the beach now and turned to look back the way they had come. There were signs of movement among their group now.

'We'd better get back,' Jem said.

As they went, he began to talk of future plans he was working on that involved the setting up of a new headquarters somewhere in the area. 'Roslarren would be perfect,' he said. 'Sadly, there's not anything suitable available at the moment.'

His words sounded a little disturbing and Harriet couldn't help thinking of what Dawna had said about her cousin's disappointment at Roslarren House not coming onto the market.

She quickened her pace, eager now to be back with the others.

# 5

The wind was whistling round the house when Harriet opened her eyes early next morning. Where had that come from? She jumped out of bed to look out of the window, expecting to see lowering clouds. Instead the sky was a hazy blue like yesterday, but conditions were definitely different. Far out she could see huge waves rolling towards the shore. Rick would be happy about that, she thought. There would be plenty of action down there today.

Indoors there was no sound of movement, but she couldn't stay in bed. She wanted to be out there in the fresh breezy air with the beach all to herself.

To her surprise there were several vehicles parked at the bottom of the slope. One of them had a surfboard still in position on its roof rack. Another had a towel draped over the bonnet. So

47

there were keen surfers out there already, early as it was?

With the tide out there was a huge expanse of beach. She didn't go down on the sand but took to the coast path that led to the top of the cliffs to get a better view. She saw at once that the surfers out there were not beginners. Fascinated at their prowess, she stopped to watch one of them take a wave just at the right moment and come zooming into shore. Others were doing the same, twisting and turning to get the utmost thrust from the force of the water. It looked magnificent.

'Great, isn't it?'

She spun round. 'Chloë!'

'I saw you come out. I can't wait to get out there too.'

'Nor me,' said Harriet.

'Rick said a lot of surfers start early every day, and I wanted to see what they looked like.'

'They seem so effortless, don't they?'

'Rick says we'll soon get the hang of it.'

'I hope so.'

Chloë laughed. 'I mean to, anyway.'

Harriet had no doubt that she would. She envied her enthusiasm and confidence. Somehow seeing those people out there now, all so efficient and dedicated, was daunting.

'Look there's a huge wave coming now,' Chloë cried. 'Oh, he's missed it!'

One of the surfers had got to his feet too late and now was in the water, soon back on his board waiting for the next opportunity to leap upright and get going.

'I can't stop watching them, can you?' said Chloë.

'We'll have to,' said Harriet. 'The others will be up by now. And we need to have breakfast and get down to the beach.'

Chloë turned away with reluctance. 'I wish we could be in two places at once.' As they went she chatted happily about buying her own board as soon as she could afford it. 'An advanced one, of course. I mean to be advanced as soon as I can. And then I'll move down to Roslarren to live for the rest of my life.'

'But what would you do?' Harriet asked.

'Surf of course.'

'I mean to earn your living?'

'I'd find something,' said Chloe airily. 'I've done lots of different things. I'd get taken on in a café or something.'

If Dawna were with them, Harriet thought, she would point out that out of season many places would close down and there wouldn't be temporary work on offer. The surf school wouldn't be busy either, of course. Rick needed to have his courses fully booked during the summer months to make up for a quiet time in the winter.

She quickened her pace, aware that she had lingered out here too long. There was work to be done. She needed to pin Rick down to set a time aside for business matters, since she was here to see to that side of things.

\* \* \*

Later, kitted out and assembled on the beach, the air of anticipation among the group was catching. Rick ran through the safety precautions again, followed by a quick practice of the pop-ups, and then they were wading out into the sea. From this angle the waves looked huge. Harriet felt a moment's panic as she knelt on her board, waiting for the right moment that never came. At each missed opportunity she was plunged off, gasping and spluttering. But she wouldn't give up. Time and again she tried, and at last she remained upright for long enough to appreciate the out-of-the world sensation that was truly invigorating.

By lunchtime everyone was too exhausted to do anything else but flop down on the beach. Dawna arrived soon afterwards, as arranged, with a double supply of pasties she had collected on the way.

'A genius suggestion on your part, Dawna,' Harriet said with gratitude as she took the one handed to her.

'You've had a good morning, yes?'

There was a chorus of agreement.

Harriet took a bite of her pasty and the meaty aroma lingered in the air in a satisfactory way. 'I needed that,' she said.

Dawna sat down beside her. 'How did it go?'

Harriet wrinkled her nose at her. 'I'll never be a champion.'

'So your plans to become a qualified instructor are on hold for the moment?'

'Where they always have been, as you well know. I'm the administrator, remember. I leave all the physical stuff to you and Rick.'

'Not much physical stuff involved in the surf shop.'

'But business is good?'

Dawna smiled. 'Booming. I just can't keep away from you lot, that's all. But I'll have to get back and relieve Jem or I'll be in trouble.'

'Jem's looking after the shop?' Harriet's heart quickened. She had imagined him miles away, surveying some inaccessible cliffs while an admiring group stood on the beach below trying to take in his windblown words.

'Under protest.'

'But I thought . . . '

'That he was leading one of the geology trails today? The group had to cancel at the last minute. Apparently there's a bug going around so it couldn't be helped. They'll book again, though. Who would turn down a wonderful chance to rise at the crack of dawn to look at some boring cliffs?'

Harriet smiled. 'Why did it have to be so early?' she said.

'The tide has to be especially low and today was perfect for that. A window of opportunity, apparently. When he told me he'd be in this area instead doing some publicity work or something, I nabbed him at once. That's why I told Rick I'd be on lunch duty for you.'

'A relief for me, I can tell you.'

'I thought it would be.'

Dawna left soon after that, and after a suitable lapse of time Rick had them all back in the water. Harriet, though, knew she couldn't stay with them for long. She had a meal to get into the slow cooker ready for the evening. Rick couldn't argue with that.

'See you down here afterwards then,' he said.

'Maybe. I'll sort a few things in the office, check for more bookings on your laptop and confirm dates.'

But he had turned away, eager to get going again. Chloë, at his side, turned to wave as they walked down the beach.

Harriet picked up her board and set off. She wasn't at all sure she would return this afternoon. She needed time to absorb the business side of things. She wondered, though, if she wasn't using this as an excuse.

\* \* \*

There were no more bookings when she checked the email, not even casual enquiries, and that was disturbing. Harriet sat back on her chair and stared at the silent telephone on the table beside the laptop. Rick had told her there was a poster in the tourist office and another in Dawna's shop. The local paper carried an advertisement too. This needed looking into, but first she needed to skin the chicken thighs to prepare them for the recipe she had in mind. This involved coating them in seasoned flour and browning them in the frying pan with onions and mushrooms. Chicken stock would be added to raisins soaked in sherry combined with sliced apple and flaked almonds. As she transferred the whole lot to the slow cooker and switched it on, she made a mental note of ingredients to buy for tomorrow's meal while in town.

She found the tourist office easily. If there was a poster here advertising Breaking Waves, she couldn't see it.

'On the wall over there,' the girl behind the desk told her when she asked. 'We had an enquiry about it this morning.'

'You did?'

'He wanted to know all we could tell him, which wasn't much, actually.'

There wasn't much on the small poster either, Harriet saw. And what there was didn't look inspiring. She couldn't imagine any would-be surfer being attracted by it. She certainly wouldn't be.

'Have you been given any handouts about it?'

'You want to learn?'

'Not much,' said Harriet.

The girl laughed. 'Me neither.'

'I'm looking for custom and we're not getting much.'

'You're working at Breaking Waves?'

'As publicity officer, among other things.'

'Just a minute. I'll check the accommodation file.' The girl ran her hand down a page of the book she got down from a shelf. 'Breaking Waves, here it is. Accommodation for twenty people max on a full-board basis. Surfing tuition. Sounds good if you like that kind of thing.'

'We need a better designed poster,' said Harriet. 'I'll see to it as soon as I can.'

Before she did so, she had a look in a few other places but couldn't locate any posters for Breaking Waves. This was bad. She bought a local paper and checked that. Yes, here it was, but as uninspiring as the poster in the tourist office. What was Rick thinking about? Or Dawna either, come to that.

The Surf Shop was the obvious place to check, since she would pass it on the way back.

'Publicity?' said Dawna when Harriet asked her. 'Rick's been seeing to that. I've designed a page for him on my website though. That's where three of the present group got to hear about Breaking Waves.'

'That was good of you,' said Harriet.

'Fine for a temporary measure, but you need your own website really.'

Harriet nodded, deep in thought. There was work to be done here if Rick wanted Breaking Waves to be a success.

Dawna turned to serve a customer. As she wrapped the item and took payment, Jem came in. He looked surprised to see Harriet.

'Not riding the waves with the best of them?'

'Hardly.'

'She hasn't time to play this afternoon,' said Dawna. 'She's researching publicity for Breaking Waves and not finding much.'

Jem raised his eyebrows. 'No? A basic requirement, I would have thought.'

Of course it was. Harriet agreed with him on that. All the same, his manner annoyed her. She wondered that Dawna didn't pick up on it.

Jem glanced round the shop. 'I see there's some publicity in here,' he said.

Harriet had noticed the colourful poster on the wall decorated with pictures of surfers swooping into shore on high breakers. This was much more attractive than the one in the tourist office. 'Did you do that, Dawna?' she asked with interest.

'It makes a bit of a splash,' Dawna said and then giggled.

'It's good.'

'My cousin's nothing if not artistic,' Jem said, smiling.

Dawna made a face at him. 'If you say so. But I have to say the poster's all Rick's work, not mine. Great, isn't it?'

'Rick must have had second thoughts about the first one he produced and designed another,' said Harriet.

'Could be.'

'We need to have more posters like that in prominent places around town, and I haven't seen any,' said Harriet.

'Not a good way to go on if you're trying to attract customers,' Jem agreed.

'Rick will have it on his laptop,' said Dawna.

Harriet frowned, disliking the tone of censure in Jem's voice. 'I shall print some out at once,' she said. 'I think I can cope.'

He looked at her gravely as if he thought she wouldn't be up to it.

'Leave her alone, Jem,' Dawna said.

'The girl only arrived yesterday. Give her a chance.'

'I'm concerned that opportunities are being missed, that's all.'

Harriet bit her lip to avoid a sharp retort. This was none of his business and he should keep out of it. She wished he would go.

'I must be off,' he said as if he could read her thoughts.

Dawna looked disappointed. 'Oh, but I thought . . . '

He smiled briefly at her. 'Another time perhaps.'

As the door closed behind him, Dawna gathered some papers on her desk into a neat pile. Her face was paler than usual and she didn't smile.

'Was that my fault?' said Harriet.

Dawna looked up. 'How could it be?'

Harriet didn't know, but the atmosphere seemed strained. With a heavy heart, she left soon after that.

# 6

After their evening meal all the others except Steven went into Newquay for an evening's entertainment. Harriet also chose to stay behind and was now seated in front of Rick's laptop.

She gazed at the screen in satisfaction. Rick's artistic skills couldn't be bettered in this one, even if his ideas of publicising the courses Breaking Waves had on offer were suspect. But that was going to change now. Determined to push Jem's critical remarks to the back of her mind, she put several sheets of paper into the printer tray ready for business.

But a vision of Jem in his crimson jersey standing in Dawna's shop wouldn't go away. She felt again her annoyance at his implied criticism of Breaking Waves that was somehow mixed with an interest in him she couldn't understand. It was increasingly clear that he resented Rick's presence in Roslarren. True, he had wanted to purchase Roslarren House, but surely there were other properties in the area? Even Dawna, his cousin, was supporting Rick's enterprise.

But back to work. She printed out one copy of the poster to see how it looked and then held it up at eye level, imagining it on the wall of one of the local cafés. Brilliant! It would work in even smaller format, too, for hand-outs to be left in suitable places such as the tourist office.

'Could you use some help?' Steven asked from the open doorway of the office.

'Take a look at this,' she said. putting the print-out flat on the table.

He came into the room and stood behind her. 'Mmn. Not bad. Colourful. You could pick that out from outer space.'

Harriet laughed. 'That's the big idea.'

He bent to examine the print more closely. Then he let out a whistle. 'Hey, wait a minute. Take a look at this.'

Harriet peered at where his finger pointed and then gazed at him in dismay. 'Am I reading it right?' she said.

'I can't believe it either. All the details are here sure enough. The tuition on offer from Beginner to Advanced. A piece about the daily sessions being adjusted to suit your needs.'

'That sound s good, doesn't it?'

'Apart from the price,' he said. 'I wouldn't consider paying that without accommodation provided, and there's no mention of that.'

He was right. There wasn't.

'We can soon make suitable changes. Like me to do it? Child's play for a computer expert like myself.' He grinned at her and she smiled back. There was something reassuring about Steven. She was glad he had stayed behind.

'It was clever of you to notice,' she said. It was odd that it hadn't been picked up before. She thought of Jem leaving the surf shop abruptly yesterday afternoon and Dawna's obvious disappointment at his abrupt departure. Neither of them had noticed the important omission either, and that was strange.

The alteration was soon done. Steven's wording made the tuition price at Breaking Waves sound reasonable and she told him so.

'So how did you hear about Breaking Waves, Steven?' she said. 'Did you surf the net?'

He laughed. 'Something like that.'

'We need our own website. I'll talk to Rick about it when I get a chance.'

'Designing them is my job,' he said. 'I'd be glad to help if you need it. You have my contact details.'

'That's good of you.'

'A pity you can't print A2 size. There must be a stationer's locally who could do some large ones. Like me to have a look?'

'Please.'

He seated himself at the desk and moments later had a result.

'I'll see to it tomorrow,' she said.

The phone rang. They both jumped.

'Thanks, Steven,' she mouthed as he closed the door quietly behind him.

The voice on the other end sounded fainter than usual and it took a moment for Harriet to recognise Rick's father. 'Derek!' she said with pleasure.

'That must be Harriet.' He paused to cough. 'And how's my boy getting on down there in Cornwall? A lot better having you there, I suspect.'

Harriet laughed. 'You must ask Rick that.'

'And he wouldn't admit it, now, would he? So where is he?'

'He's gone into town with the group.'

'And left you behind?'

'My choice. There's some work I have to do.'

'At this time of night?'

Harriet glanced at her watch. 'It's only half past eight.'

'Almost my bedtime.' He coughed again.

'How are you, Derek? You don't sound too good.'

'A bit of a health issue, that's all.

Nothing to worry about. I feel better for knowing you're there, Harriet my dear. But don't let him work you too hard while he skives off enjoying himself.'

Laughing, she promised she wouldn't and that she would get Rick to ring back in the morning. Derek was interested in her account of the surfing lessons down on the beach and the barbecue they had all enjoyed.

As she replaced the receiver she wondered exactly what these health issues were and how serious. He had always made light of any problems in the past, but if anything was wrong Rick should know about it. Perhaps his father would confide in him in the morning.

★   ★   ★

The wind had dropped next day and the surf was magnificent. No one needed urging to get breakfast over and done with quickly so they could get down there into the water. No one except Harriet.

'The posters can wait,' Rick said. 'We

won't get better surf than this, Harriet. Why waste time messing about in town when you could be out on the water enjoying yourself?'

That was the whole point. She wouldn't be enjoying herself in huge waves like today. But she couldn't tell him that. Instead she shrugged and tried to look suitably resigned. 'Needs must, Rick. I'm here to help, after all. What would your dad say if he knew I'd neglected something important?'

'Dad? He'd see the sense of you becoming proficient so you could help out with the tuition.'

'You *have* rung him, haven't you, Rick?'

'Ah.'

'I said you would.'

'We're in a bit of a hurry. Later will do. Could you phone and tell him that, if you're not coming with us?'

She could promise little else but she didn't like it. 'This evening then?' she said. 'I'll tell him that.'

'And you'll put in the pasty order for lunch?'

'Same as yesterday. I'll collect and deliver them myself. One o'clock?'

'On the instant.'

'As if. But if you're not out of the water then I'll eat them all myself.'

He grinned. 'You wouldn't dare!'

'Just try me, that's all.'

Derek Seton sounded unsurprised when he heard her voice and the reason for her call. 'I take it my son's more interested in getting into the surf than in talking to his old dad?'

'It's especially good today, apparently.'

'Well as long are things are going well, my dear.'

'Of course,' she said, relieved that he had taken it so well. 'You must come and see for yourself soon, Derek.'

He chuckled. 'I might just do that. A surfing lesson or two would be just the job.'

Harriet smiled as she put down the phone. It would be good to see him again. His apparent weakness when they spoke last night had worried her, but this morning his voice sounded far stronger and that was good.

She found the stationer's easily enough and waited while her printing order was carried out. Then she took one of the larger posters into Dawna's surf shop to replace the one with the incorrect information.

'And I didn't even notice,' Dawna marvelled.

Any doubts Harriet had were dispelled in an instant. Ashamed that she had wondered even for a moment that she might have done and not mentioned it for whatever reason, Harriet said, 'You're a good friend to Rick, Dawna.'

Dawna flushed. 'What brought that on?'

'This and that.'

There were one or two likely customers wandering round the shop now and Dawna turned to attend to them. While she was doing so, Harriet inspected the rack of wetsuits, wondering whether or not to invest in one herself. But the price made her stop short. She hadn't taken in the hire charge incorporated in Rick's inclusive package for the week, but it must be fairly steep. When she got back she would create a spreadsheet for a clear record of expenditure and profit. Rick had handed her a box of receipts but so far there had been little time to see to it. This must be done immediately.

Rick had transported Harriet's board with the rest so all she had to do was to take the pasties for lunch and a cool bag of oranges and bananas down with her when it was time.

The others were there waiting, which surprised her. They looked subdued as they sat about on the sand, as if the morning had gone badly after their high expectations at breakfast time.

'Something wrong?' said Harriet.

'There was a panic half an hour ago,' Anna told her as she set down her baggage. 'A body-boarder strayed out of his area and got hit.'

'But not by one of us,' Neil hastened to assure her.

'Bad enough,' said Rick.

'All the safety precautions we keep hearing about certainly make sense,' Steven said.

Rick nodded. 'The chap was at fault. He has the lifeguards to thank it wasn't worse. He got caught up in the safety cord and was dragged under.'

Chloë shivered. 'That poor girl on the surfboard. I'm glad it wasn't me,' she said.

'She got straight back out there as soon as she saw he was going to be okay,' said Rick. 'The right thing to do, of course. If you don't do it you're finished. You'll never want to surf again.'

'I can understand that,' said Harriet.

'Me too,' said Anna.

'Food?' said Rick. 'Who's hungry?'

They fell on the pasties with eagerness, taking two apiece and holding one in each hand. Harriet smiled. It was good to see it after the lethargy that had surprised her when she arrived.

'That was good,' said Mark, wiping his mouth with the back of his hand.

Harriet unzipped the cool bag. 'An orange?'

'Thanks.'

'Drinks all round?' said Rick, springing up. 'I'll get them organised.'

He was soon back from the kiosk.

The afternoon's session went well. Rick started with safety precautions as usual, and then some extra-strenuous exercises. By the time they were finished Harriet was as keen to get in the water as anyone. Three times she managed to get up on her board and remain there for seconds each time. She waited for Anna, who had had a longer run, and they lay face-down on their boards and paddled out together to wait for the next suitable wave.

'Here it comes!' called Mark from close by.

Once more Harriet wasn't quick enough to gauge the right moment. She waited for the next wave and then the next. In the end she lay face-down on her board and floated, enjoying the gentle movement of the water but clinging on tightly so that as the next wave came she was taken with it into shore. This was more like it. This was what the body-boarders enjoyed in their own much larger area of sea, and with smaller and lighter boards it would be so much easier to manage. She got to her feet and waded back out as far as she could before she saw the next wave coming. Then she did the same again.

This time when she stood up in shallow water she looked around for the others, hoping Rick hadn't noticed what she was doing. It was some moments before she picked him out riding a wave at the same time as Chloë.

She had no idea what the time was but the sun was lower in the sky now. She turned away and walked out of the sea until she reached the warm sand. For a few minutes more she stood and watched the surfers. Time enough to see that Rick never left Chloë's side.

Once or twice, others of their group looked around for him. Needing help and encouragement? Possibly. But it was clear to Harriet that he wasn't there for them, only for Chloë.

And that wasn't good enough.

# 7

Harriet left her board close to the cool bag and the rest of their belongings as a message to Rick that she was out of the water and off to the house, where further duties awaited her.

It was difficult not to feel frustration at Rick's behaviour. The others were bound to resent his lack of attention. How could they help it? His father would be as appalled at Rick's lack of professionalism as she was herself.

She thought of Steven's offer to assist in the setting up of a website for Breaking Waves. She hadn't had the chance to discuss this with Rick yet. It needed thinking about, because she didn't know what costs would be involved.

The phone rang as she switched on the laptop. An enquiry for lessons! She dotted down the details with mounting optimism. The caller was a local girl wanting surfing lessons at weekends.

'No problem,' Harriet said cheerfully. 'Rick will get back to you to confirm the booking the minute he gets in. Yes, ten o'clock on Saturday morning. I look forward to meeting you.'

This was good. There were two more days yet before Saturday, and with luck there would be more bookings. The present group would be leaving Breaking Waves by then, and tuition for a couple of lessons down on the beach while Harriet was preparing the accommodation for the next influx — if there was one — would be perfect for Rick. She hoped he would think so.

When Rick came at last, he was full of enthusiasm for the day's events. Harriet met him in the yard at the back of the house.

'Perfect conditions,' he said, unzipping his wetsuit. 'What a day! Chloe's progress is great. I left them all down there. Gluttons for punishment, I told them. I've got to phone Dad.'

'And someone else, too, as soon as

you've changed,' Harriet told him. 'You'll never guess, Rick. A booking for the day on Saturday. I said you'd confirm.'

'A booking on Saturday?' he said.

'For surfing lessons.'

'But Chloë . . . '

'*Chloë?*' Harriet cried. 'What's Chloë got to do with it? She's not the only one. And the sooner you realise it, the better, or you'll have a rebellion on your hands, and . . . ' She broke off, her voice trembling.

He looked at her, appalled. 'What's got into you all of a sudden, Harriet?'

'You have. You're so laid-back it isn't true.'

'Me? You've got that wrong.'

'You're ignoring Steven and the others.'

'Have they complained?'

'No they haven't, not yet.'

'Well then?'

'But I saw for myself what you're doing, and it's not good enough. They've paid good money too. They deserve just as much attention as Chloë's getting.'

'But Saturday . . . '

'D'you want me to phone up this poor girl and cancel?'

'You're over-reacting, Harriet. I'll get Dawna to help out.'

'You won't. She's got a shop to run. Saturday's a busy day.'

'Her assistant will cope.'

The sheer arrogance of this astounded her. Where was his enthusiasm for the success of Breaking Waves now?

He glared at her as if all this was her doing. She didn't know how to convince him that they needed the goodwill of everyone who booked at Breaking Waves. They needed good reviews and recommendations, not the feeling from clients that unless they were young and pretty they would be sidelined.

'You'll get your chance to have a go again tomorrow, Harriet, if that's what's bothering you,' he said.

Seething, she managed not to react. A slanging match between the two of them was not the way to go. The others might appear at any moment, and who else might join in then?

'So will you phone her and confirm?' she said.

'If you insist. And Dad too.'

'Thank goodness for that.'

He smiled suddenly and ran a hand through his damp hair. 'Stop fussing, Harriet. Everything's going to work out fine.'

She had to be content with that.

To her surprise, Rick had found time during the day to use his smartphone to capture the progress of all of them on film at various stages. So the evening was spent watching the results on the small laptop screen and then running them through again and again so they could be analysed.

'This is a brilliant way to pick up on what we're doing wrong,' Anna murmured.

'A valuable way,' Steven agreed.

Neil leaned forward to get a better look. 'Wow, that was the right moment catching that wave like that.'

'That's you,' said Rick, grinning.

'Unbelievable,' said Neil, gratified.

They all stared at the small screen,

fascinated, even though there were a few laughs and amusing comments when things didn't go quite right.

'I can't believe I did that,' said Mark in disgust when he saw himself misjudging the wave and falling headfirst off his board.

'If the leash hadn't been attached securely you'd have parted company for sure,' Neil said.

'Best to see it for yourself, don't you agree? Now look . . . ' Rick pointed out the correct procedure and the others listened avidly.

This was Rick at his best, Harriet thought, leaning back her chair behind the others. He was appreciating each in turn, dwelling on their good points and sympathising when they didn't get it quite right. Then he invited them all to add their comments to what he said and listened carefully when they did so.

'Notice the way Chloë leans into the movement,' he said. 'There she goes.'

Mark whistled in appreciation. 'How does the girl do it?'

'Easy if you're not a complete idiot,' said Chloë, ducking behind Anna for protection.

Mark laughed. 'Just listen to her!'

Harriet smiled. It was all good-natured, and great to listen to them. 'Fancy a hot drink, anyone?' she said at last.

There was a chorus of orders for tea, coffee and hot chocolate.

'And bring some of that fruitcake,' said Rick. 'I'm starving.'

'After that mammoth plateful of chicken curry you put away?' said Chloë. 'I can't believe that.'

He grinned at her. 'Hungry work dealing with you lot.'

'And hungry work taking everything in, let alone putting it into practice,' said Mark. 'Can we have another run-through?'

'D'you want some help, Harriet?' Anna asked, getting up.

Harriet was glad of her company, especially as she had the feeling that Anna wasn't quite as keen on continuous surf-talk as some of them.

Anna got the mugs out of the cupboard and put them on the tray while Harriet filled the kettle and took the milk out of the fridge.

'Do you like surfing, Harriet?' Anna said.

Harriet paused in the process of pouring milk into a pan. 'Not as much as I thought I would,' she admitted. 'But it's early days yet and I have high hopes that things will change.'

'I wish I didn't find it so hard to learn,' said Anna.

'But we all learn at different rates,' said Harriet. 'If it was easy, places like Breaking Waves would go out of business because they wouldn't be necessary.'

'I hadn't thought of that.'

'You seem to me to be someone who has plenty of patience.'

'Well yes, for some things. But with everyone else being so good it shows me up.'

'Has Rick said that?'

'No, of course not. Rick's kind.'

'And honest. He'd tell you if he

thought you'd never be any good. Give it time, Anna and you'll get there.'

'But Chloë picked it up so quickly.'

'With a lot of help.'

Anna was silent for a moment. 'I noticed that,' she said quietly.

Harriet spooned instant coffee in to three of the mugs. 'That'll change, I promise you.'

By the time all the drinks were ready to be carried in, fifteen minutes had passed. 'Sorry to take so long,' Harriet said as Anna held the door open for her.

Steven got up and took the laden tray from her and put it on the table. 'Who's for hot chocolate?' he asked.

'We haven't been wasting our time,' said Rick, looking pleased with himself.

'The magic of technology,' said Neil.

'What d'you think, Harriet?' said Rick. 'I've just placed an order online for a large-screen TV for in here. We need it, as you can see. We'll be able to watch all the action then and it'll make all the difference.'

'But how much..?' she began, and stopped at the expression on Rick's face. This was not the moment for a discussion of finances. He beamed round at them all.

'Too bad it's not being delivered till Friday,' Neil said. 'I'd have have liked to have seen myself full-size immediately.'

'I can't believe the screen will be that size,' Mark said, grinning. 'You could always look in the mirror.'

They all laughed and Harriet tried to join in, but she was deeply disappointed at what Rick had done. All the large TV screens in the world wouldn't be much use if they had no more bookings coming in, and their own lack of a website might have a lot to do with that.

Maybe she was being unduly pessimistic and they would be able to set up their own website as well. She wondered what Dawna would say about it and wished, suddenly, she was here with them. Harriet needed her calm common sense to help her see this in perspective.

# 8

Rain, rain and more rain! Who would believe it? In dismay, Harriet gazed at the raindrops sliding down the window. With the poor visibility she could hardly see the beach and the cliffs beyond.

'Our last-but-one day,' Chloë moaned at breakfast as she poured cereal into a bowl and added milk.

'What's the problem?' said Mark.

'We'll be wet anyway.' Anna shuddered.

'It'll ease off,' said Rick with confidence. 'No one wants to pull out of a lesson, do they?' He glanced at Harriet.

'Of course not,' she said, smiling. 'And I can't wait to see what sort of a fool I look at our analysing session at the laptop this evening.'

Everyone laughed.

She had gone off to bed early last night, not trusting herself to keep quiet about his latest purchase. He must have known her true reaction because he had kept out of her way so far this morning.

'I think someone should film Rick in action,' said Anna.

'Definitely,' said Harriet. 'Can I volunteer?'

'Will we still have a barbecue?' said Chloë.

'In the rain?' said Neil.

Rick, laughing, held his hands over his ears. 'Too many questions,' he said. 'Wait and see.'

The rain had eased a little by the time they were ready for the beach and the clouds were already clearing from the horizon. Like yesterday, the surf was good and Rick's spirits were high.

Harriet hadn't heard about the barbecue for this evening. Plans must have been made after she had retired to bed. It wasn't a bad idea if weather permitted. There was plenty of suitable food in the freezer and she could pick up a supply of bread rolls when she collected the pasties for lunch.

The usual preparatory procedures were attended to and then they were soon in the water after a long walk across hard, wet sand to reach it. They were all keen to correct mistakes and practice more manoeuvres. Harriet was pleased to see that Rick spent time with everyone, helping and encouraging. She had moments of exhilaration herself, remaining upright for seconds at a time.

The morning passed quickly. As directed, she collected Rick's smartphone from the house on her way back from the pasty shop as well as checking the answer phone in case there were more bookings. None.

Rick did the filming first, making sure he concentrated on everyone. Then, seeing Harriet, he handed the phone to her. 'Your turn now,' he said.

'I'll make the most of it,' she promised. It wasn't altogether easy because of the speed involved, but she got several good shots.

'Hide it among our things,' Rick said

at last. 'It'll be okay. Then come back in and join us.'

Harriet wasn't too sure of the wisdom of this. She looked around carefully on reaching base. Then she saw a family of four coming across the beach towards her . . . a man and a woman and two teenage children all in shorts and bright T-shirts.

The man smiled as they got close. 'We've been watching you all,' he said. 'Obviously you're giving surfing lessons. 'We're keen to learn ourselves.'

'It looks fun, Dad,' said the girl, while the boy nodded in approval.

'You've come to the right place,' said Harriet. 'Are you on holiday?'

'A fortnight. This is our first week.'

They needed a board up nearby advertising Breaking Waves, Harriet thought. Another publicity opportunity almost lost. She would make sure they had one to place near them on the sand each day. 'I hope you're having a good time,' she said.

'Definitely. But it'll be even better if

we can learn to surf too. Lucky we saw you coming back up here. Taking photos, were you?'

'Rick — that's our qualified instructor — likes to get the results up on screen in the evenings so the students can see themselves in action. It's a good way for picking up on faults.'

'Brilliant idea,' said the boy.

Harriet smiled. 'We're the Breaking Wave Surf School and our headquarters are up there. You can see the house from here.'

'A fine situation.'

'We run weekly courses with accommodation.'

'And meals?' said the boy.

'Oh yes, meals too. Usually lunch on the beach, but a good solid meal every evening.'

'And breakfast?'

'Stop it, Simon,' his father ordered.

'Breakfast too,' Harriet said, smiling at him. 'And barbecues in the evening sometimes. The group at the moment are having an all-inclusive holiday, but we do daily lessons too, starting on Saturday.'

'That would suit us fine, wouldn't it, Denise?' said the man of the family. 'A day to try it out and see if we like it. Can we book ourselves in for this Saturday?'

Harriet, delighted with the way things were going, gave details of times and prices. 'I take it you can all swim?' she said.

Denise laughed. 'Like seals, these two, and their mum and dad aren't bad.'

'Then consider it booked. Now what about equipment?'

'We've got wetsuits but we haven't got boards.'

'No problem. We have boards for hire and I'll see that suitable ones are down here for you. Could you get here early so we can get the business part over and be ready to start at ten o'clock?'

'We'll be here,' they chorused.

'I'll look forward to seeing you.'

She was smiling as they walked back

across the beach. That made five people booked for the Saturday lesson. Perfect.

She was still holding the smartphone and looked for somewhere to hide it among their belongings, but she didn't feel like getting back in the water now. Maybe she'd go up to the house and get some things ready for the barbecue, since the weather had changed for the better. No sign of rain now, and the headland to the north was looking hazy in the afternoon light. A good sign.

She ran down to where she had left her board, picked it up and waved to Rick, whom she saw looking at her. He waved back, guessing her intentions.

★   ★   ★

'I wish I could come too,' said Dawna. Her voice on the phone sounded regretful. 'Jem's coming over. He wants to discuss something important. He says he needs my input.'

Harriet thought briefly of her first evening, when Jem had come to find his cousin to ask her something, and wondered what it was. The man was a mass of secrets. She wondered that he didn't trip over them. 'There'll be other barbecues,' she said.

'But not with this group. Ah well, it can't be helped.'

'And I've got something to tell you, Dawna. Two things — one good, one bad. At least, I think so.'

'Come on then, spill.'

'Rick's ordered a television with a massive screen for the dining room so we can view the images in action.'

'Is that good or bad?'

'It costs. A lot.'

'Ah.'

'That's all very well, Dawna, but I gather it's top-of-the-range. Ridiculous before we're certain of being financially secure. And we haven't even got our own website yet. What sort of business are we running without that?'

'I get your point.'

'The set's being delivered on Friday.'

'So a big celebration?'

'A welcome party's been suggested.'

'What d'you feel about that?'

'Pleased, I suppose. About the party, I mean. There will be plenty of food to be eaten up. Mark suggested roasting an ox but I don't think he was serious.'

Dawna laughed. 'I wish I could come too, but I've been booked for the evening. Or I've booked *him* as a thank-you for guarding the shop.'

'Jem?'

'Who else? We're attending a dinner together at the Mount Tor Hotel in Falmouth. But I'll try and make him book a surfing lesson with Breaking Waves. It's time he learnt to surf. But he won't agree this time either, of course.'

Harriet felt a frisson of pleasure at the thought. They needed more bookings, but there was something else here, too, that she would think about later.

'And the good thing?' said Dawna.

'Four bookings for lessons on Saturday as well as the one we had yesterday. A family on holiday. Oh and Dawna, I think we should have a board with the poster attached that we stick into the sand when we're down on the beach to advertise what we're doing.'

'Genius.'

'I'll check the regulations.'

'Good for you.'

'And I'll be starting surfing lessons again on Saturday with basics too,' Harriet said. 'That can't be a bad thing.'

'You'll be a qualified instructor before we know it.'

Harriet laughed as she put down the phone. Dawna was good for her with her optimistic approach to life.

★ ★ ★

Mark and Neil took over the barbecuing that evening, larking about and pretending to burn the pork chops as the others egged them on. Harriet sat with her back against a rock watching the proceedings, her part in the preparation done.

It should have been a happy occasion, but there was an underlying sadness in the air. The week was coming to an end, and with it the thought that most of them wouldn't see each other again when they dispersed the day after tomorrow.

Even though it would soon be high tide, with a smaller area of beach than the other evening, there was room enough for a game of volleyball. But no one seemed inclined to move after they had finished eating.

Harriet glanced at the cliffs further along that Jem had found so fascinating. They looked gloomy in the fading light. She thought of Dawna and her cousin enjoying each other's company, dining at the hotel in Falmouth, and felt a stab of envy.

She was aware now of sniffs and a loud gulp. Chloë sat nearby with her arms round her legs and her head bent over her knees. Her shoulders were shaking.

Harriet moved closer. 'Chloë, what's wrong?'

Chloe lifted her tear-stained face. 'I can't bear it!'

'We've another day tomorrow. The week's not over yet.'

But Chloë wouldn't be consoled. Rick, noticing, got up and came to her. He caught hold of her hands. 'Come on, up you get. The night's not over yet. We'll go off to Newquay and see a bit of life, you and me. 'What d'you say to that?'

She brightened at once. 'You mean it?' she said.

'Come on, before the others notice.'

But Harriet had noticed all too clearly. With dismay, she watched them go jauntily across the sand.

Suddenly she felt ready for bed.

# 9

The television set arrived late in the afternoon when Harriet was beginning to give up hope. Not that she was looking forward to its arrival, but she had been up here at the house since lunchtime, and there was nothing much to do now that she had organised the party food for tonight except check the emails every half hour or so in the hope there might be more enquiries and bookings.

The box looked enormous and Harriet looked at it in horror. The young man delivering it carried it into the dining room as if it was full of feathers. 'So you do surfing lessons up here then, do you?' he said as he put it down on the floor. 'I saw your board.'

'We have surfing lessons on the beach and in the water.'

He grinned. 'Who would have thought that?'

'Are you interested?' she asked, smiling too.

'Might be, my mate and me. We moved the business down here last autumn so we've been busy since.'

'Then let me give you one of our leaflets.' Luckily there was a pile handy.

He looked carefully at the one she handed him. 'So what does it say, then? We don't have to live in?'

'Not if you live locally. We do daily lessons, morning and afternoon, especially at weekends. And evenings too, by arrangement.' She had surprised herself with that last addition, but why not?

'And there's a phone number?'

'At the bottom.'

'So, we'll get back to you. That's a promise.'

It was a surprise too, she thought as he tucked the leaflet in the back pocket of his jeans and then left. All publicity was welcome, and who knew where this might lead?

Rick came in soon after, having seen the delivery van from the beach. 'Where is it then?' he demanded, his eyes bright and his hair damp against his head.

Harriet looked at his sandy footprints on the bare boards.

'Yes, I know,' he said impatiently. 'No time to change. This is an important moment.'

She couldn't deny that from the way he was tearing at the cardboard lid of the box. 'Shall I get one of the knives from the kitchen?' she said.

'No need.' He ripped the box open. 'Steven's just following me up. He'll be here in a minute. Can you help me lift it out?'

The television set didn't look as enormous as Harriet feared when they placed it on the floor. Rick stood back and looked at it proudly. 'It's just what we need.' Harriet said nothing. Rick looked at her quickly and away again. 'Now don't be like that. It's an investment.'

An expensive one, she thought. But what was done was done and she must make the best of it. There had just been a hint of more bookings and they weren't quite destitute yet.

Steven had taken time to change out of his wetsuit and came in soon after as keen as Rick to get the set in position and tune it in to their satisfaction. 'Wow!' he said in admiration. 'You've got a fine one here. Top-of-the-range, by the look of it.'

Rick looked pleased. 'Yep, I think so.'

While they were engrossed, Harriet took the box and all the wrapping out to the yard and put it all in one of the outhouses for recycling. Then she switched on the kettle and made coffee. She carried the tray into the room and put it down on the table.

'How's that then, Harriet?' Rick said.

'It looks good,' she said.

He beamed at her. 'Wait till you see it in action.'

By this time Steven had the laptop placed ready on a small table Rick had brought down from upstairs. Moments later the results of the day's filming were on-screen. They were certainly impressive seen like this. Rick ran through them once and then clicked on to the previous day's filming. Then he turned the television off.

'Next showing will be with the full audience,' he said as he reached for his coffee. 'Everyone will see how they've improved and go away happy. A good finish to the course.'

'A good wrapping up,' Steven agreed.

'Showers first, and party clothes, and something being done about the food. Then we'll get going,' said Rick.

'Will you be able to wait that long?' said Harriet.

He drained the last of his drink and grinned. 'Yep, I'll give it my best shot.'

The rest were late coming up from the beach and it was some time before proceedings could begin. Seated in a tight group to view the filming, they were all impressed with the progress they had made and insisted on seeing a repeat.

The girls had made a fruit punch with alcohol added at the last moment.

'Just to get us going,' said Anna.

Harriet didn't think there would be any problem with that. Spirits were high and there was an atmosphere of forced anticipation that promised a lively time. There was certainly more noise than on other evenings. Only Chloë was quiet. Once or twice Anna tried to jolly her along, but Chloë refused all attempts to get her to join in with the others. She sat in a corner of the kitchen while everyone filled their plates with the assortment of food that Harriet produced.

'Just using up all our odds and ends,' Harriet said cheerfully as she placed a large stilton and broccoli quiche in the centre of the table next to a huge pizza. She had made a bacon and leek quiche too, and there were plates of mini steak and ale pies and an assortment of cheeses. The rocket salad and bowl of tomatoes added a touch of colour. 'There's some carrot and coriander soup heating up if anyone wants it,' she said.

Neil lifted the lid of the pan on the stove and sniffed appreciatively. A warm aroma filled the room.

'If these are odds and ends, what would a full dinner party look like?' said Steven.

Harriet laughed. 'That's a good question.'

'We'll have to come back one day and find out,' said Anna.

Rick, his colour high, was refilling glasses. He took a full one over to Chloë, pulled over another chair and sat down beside her. 'You're not eating anything?'

She gazed at him, her eyes full of tears. 'I can't bear to go home tomorrow.'

His chair creaked as he moved slightly. 'We don't want to lose you lot either.'

He got up soon after that and went to join Mark and Neil who were arguing about surfing tactics, each doing his fair share of boasting.

'Leave all this to me,' Harriet said at last, waving a hand at the depleted feast. 'Last chance to enjoy yourselves. Make the most of it.'

They piled outside, even Chloë. It was dusky out there now, but Rick had the outside lights on and it was warm. Harriet could hear the muted sounds of jollity as she covered what little food remained and put it in the fridge. Then she started on the washing up. That done, she went outside too.

Chloë was the first to go off to bed, yawning and saying she had a long day ahead of her tomorrow. The rest soon followed.

Harriet, in the kitchen to check the place was tidy, made herself a last cup of coffee. She was glad of these moments of peace after a job well done. There was no doubt that the week had gone well. She and Rick could bask in a sense of achievement for a little while.

She heard a sound and the door from the hall was pushed open. 'Chloë?'

Chloë had piled her hair up with a shiny hair slide that sparkled in the electric light. 'Where's Rick?' she said.

Mark and Anna had a long journey ahead of them and were ready to leave as soon as breakfast was over next day. Steven, too, was prepared to be on his way to Bristol, taking with him a pile of leaflets and an A4 poster for his office.

Farewells were said and Anna gave Harriet a huge hug. 'You've been great, you and Rick,' she murmured, her eyes damp. 'We'll come again one day, won't we, Mark?'

'We sure will,' he said with enthusiasm as he heaved up his bulging holdall and then shook hands with Rick. 'Good luck to you and to Breaking Waves. You've been great.'

Harriet couldn't speak for a moment. These people were their first clients at Breaking Waves and she would always remember them because of that. From them she had discovered the satisfaction of working with a group. Each member had got on well with the others, too. It was hard to see them go.

'Any chance of hiring the board for a while longer?' Neil asked. 'I think I'll stick around down here for a while and get a bit more practice. I'm only going as far as Exeter.'

'Of course you can,' Harriet said, pleased.

'I'll get myself down to the beach now,' he said. 'I'm all packed up and my stuff's in the car.'

'Feel free to leave it where it is until you go,' said Rick. 'We'll see you down there, then.'

&#42; &#42; &#42;

The family of four who had booked in yesterday were early and had already introduced themselves to Rick by the time Harriet, breathless, joined them just after ten o'clock. Rick had brought down the notice board on its pole on which he had stuck one of the posters to advertise Breaking Waves. It looked good, Harriet thought. Truly professional. With luck it would attract others keen to learn.

Chloe was nowhere to be seen when Rick was ready to set off, and so Harriet had stayed behind to wait for her to appear and to say goodbye. Last night when Chloë had appeared in the kitchen in her fancy nightwear, Harriet had been brusque with her. She had assured her that Rick had gone to bed tired out and was not to be disturbed. Chloë, of course, had pouted and made a fuss. When at last she went upstairs, Harriet went with her to check that she returned to the room she shared with Anna. As an extra precaution she alerted Rick on her mobile, and from his grunts of dismay knew that he would make sure his bedroom door had the key turned in the lock.

At five minutes to ten she checked that the house was empty and there was no sign of Chloë outside either. She had probably found it easier to slip away without anyone noticing. But Rick had obviously felt this keenly and even now was tight-lipped and edgy as he introduced the five members of today's group.

'Denise and Peter Buckley, and Emily and Simon,' Rick said. And then, indicating the tall, dark girl at his side, 'This is Mandy Weir, who's not really a beginner but wants to start again with basics. We've done the business part, Harriet. So shall we make a start?'

Harriet found that being given the chance to start again with basics was helpful. She even felt eager to get into the water after some time practising pop-ups. If they should have a mixed ability group in future, she would be able to stay with the beginners to help and encourage them during the times when Rick was concentrating on the more advanced.

The lesson had been booked for two hours, and by the end of that time Harriet's gain in confidence surprised her. Because of it she had some really good runs in.

Both Denise and Peter looked exhausted, but Emily and Simon had to be persuaded to get out of the water at the end of the session and join their parents on the beach.

'I wish we had our own boards,' Emily lamented.

'You hire them out, don't you, Rick?' Peter asked.

'If you want them for the afternoon that's fine.'

'Only two,' said Denise firmly.

'The big ones?' asked Simon hopefully.

'Yep, if you want.'

'Anything for a laugh,' said their father.

Mandy, too, opted for hiring a board for the afternoon. And then Neil joined them again, pleased with his morning's practice and planning lunch in town before using the surfboard again in the afternoon.

Rick quirked an eyebrow at Harriet.

'Why bother?' he said. 'There's plenty of food up at the house, isn't there, Harriet? Come and join us.'

'You're sure?' Neil looked from one to the other.

'Of course,' said Harriet warmly,

pleased that they would be seeing more of him.

'So that's that,' Rick said as the three of them walked up to the house with their boards. 'I might be down there this afternoon too if Chloë doesn't show up.'

'Chloë?' said Neil. 'Is she still around?'

Rick shrugged. 'Who knows? She didn't say anything about her plans. Nope, she didn't say anything.'

The bitterness was still there, and Harriet could see that he was struggling hard to come to terms with it. Maybe an afternoon's surfing would be the best thing for him, especially with Neil's company. She thought of the work in the house that awaited her, but was glad that she had put off the changing of beds and the loads for the washing machine and had taken advantage of the surfing lesson this morning.

★   ★   ★

'Success, Harriet!' Dawna's voice over the phone that evening sounded triumphant.

'We had a fantastic meal at Mount Tor. How about you? Did you enjoy the party?'

'Everyone seemed to have a good time and most of the food disappeared.'

'So a good time was had by all, yes? And the massive TV?'

'A wow.'

Dawna's laugh was low and throaty. 'But you're still not happy about it?'

'Rick didn't have to go top-of-the-range. What's wrong with a cheaper one?'

'I suppose he thought it was a good investment.'

'But one we can't afford at this time. Maybe when we're up and running successfully, but not now.'

'But you've had more bookings?'

'Only for the odd lesson. But I've a feeling some of today's group will be back for more tomorrow.'

'There you are then, yes? And I've got another almost-booking for you.'

'You have?'

'For tomorrow afternoon. Is that OK?'

'Great.'

'You'll never guess. I managed to twist Jem's arm and he's coming to have a preliminary look. Brilliant or what?'

A ripple of anticipation ran through Harriet, which she quickly suppressed. It was clear that Jem had agreed only to please Dawna and she had no business to read more into it than that. 'Brilliant,' she said.

'And Rick's OK about everything?'

'Not about Chloë.'

'Chloë?' Dawna sounded alarmed.

'Well, yes. She left without saying goodbye. He's really hurt about that.'

There was a moment's silence.

'Dawna . . . are you still there?'

'I must fly. Things to do. Speak to you soon.'

Deep in thought, Harriet put the phone down.

# 10

A perfect morning with the early sunshine sparkling on the ridges of wet sand ... what could be better? Harriet felt far more cheerful about Breaking Waves's prospects this morning. Not only was a lesson for four booked for the afternoon, but Jem and Dawna would be here too. Smiling, she leaned out of her bedroom window listening to the seagulls calling from somewhere behind the house. She could almost smell the salt in the bright air. She dressed quickly and ran downstairs.

'I'll get the notice board down there straight away,' Rick said as they finished breakfast and he carried her bowl and cup over to the draining board. 'How about a bit more practice for you, Harriet, before we get busy?'

She smiled at his optimism. 'I'd love to, but later on. I want to get a few things done here first and there's a phone call to make to your father. I promised him an update every Sunday morning.'

'We need to let people see we're in business down there.'

'Good point. I'll be there as quickly as I can.'

He nodded. 'Yep. I'll get off then.'

Harriet was able to sound truly hopeful at the way things were going when she phoned Derek Seton a little while later. It was easy this sunny morning to dwell on the good things like the successful week that had just gone by. No need to mention that there had been no more enquiries for the full package and only a few bookings for the two-hour lessons.

The church bells were ringing as she walked down to the beach. Already the heat from the sun was strengthening. Because of it the beach was busy, but the Breaking Waves board stood up proudly in the area marked out for the surfers. Rick had left a rucksack near it alongside Harriet's board. It occurred to her that someone should be nearby at all times, ready to answer questions and take any bookings that might come their way. But perhaps not. It would be obvious that the people concerned were in the vicinity and would be back there soon.

She looked out to sea. Today the water was surging with black-clad figures and it was impossible to pick Rick out from among them. She hoped he was enjoying himself out there unencumbered by learners needing his attention.

'Hi there!' said a voice she recognised.

She smiled. 'Hi, Emily.'

The girl looked hopeful. 'Can we book another lesson?'

'Did your mum and dad send you?'

'They're in church but I know they want to. I saw you from over there. This afternoon?'

'Why not?' said Harriet.

'And can I use one of the big boards too?'

'You'll have to ask Rick. He's the one in charge,' Harriet said, smiling.

Emily shrugged. 'See you later, then.'

The morning was enjoyable because Rick left her alone and she could rest when she felt inclined, and not feel guilty in missing a wave because she should be an example to others. Once or twice she stopped to watch others weaving their way from side to side to make the most of the wave they were riding.

They took turns to go up to the house for something to eat and to rest up there for a while. When Harriet got back from her break Rick greeted her with the news that the leader of a youth group was interested in their residential courses and had taken one of the leaflets that he had brought down in the rucksack.

'He was definitely interested. He said he'll get back to us soon about numbers.'

'That's promising,' she said.

'Yep.'

She unzipped her wetsuit and wriggled out of it. Her yellow bikini was new and the sun on her body felt good. She had brought suntan lotion down with her this time, prepared for a sun-tanning session while Rick went up to the house.

'Your turn to get some more bookings,' he said, grinning back over his shoulder as he left.

'I wish,' she called after him.

She was almost asleep by the time he got back to the beach. She sat up and rubbed her eyes. 'Did you check the answer phone?' she asked.

'Yep, I did.'

'And?'

'Chloë.'

She looked at him in surprise. 'Chloë's been in touch?'

'She's got a job locally. She wants to know if we can put her up.'

'What sort of job?'

'At a campsite on the road out to Newquay. General dogsbody, I gather, but mostly in the camp shop.'

'Did she say why she went off without saying goodbye?'

'Nope.'

'And you didn't ask?'

'She forgot, I think.'

Harriet was silent for a moment, thinking. How could anyone forget to say goodbye, especially someone who had been the recipient of special attention as Chloë had? No, she hadn't forgotten. There was something else here going on beneath the surface.

'Anyway, it was good to hear from her,' Rick said.

'I suppose.' Surely a campsite could provide some sort of accommodation for Chloë? She must have stayed somewhere last night. If it was left to Harriet she would refuse outright, but this was Rick's problem and he must deal with it.

'What did you tell her?' she asked.

'I said we'd think about it.'

Harriet nodded. That showed a bit of sense anyway.

★　★　★

The tide was only just beginning to come in again when the afternoon's session began. So far there was no sign

118

of Jem or of Dawna. As she walked to the sea's edge with the others, Harriet kept glancing back at the beach hoping to catch a glimpse of them.

Although she was determined to work hard all afternoon, the energy of Simon and Emily was hard to keep up with. After a while Harriet stood in the shallow water with her board at her side and watched them. With a suddenness that was shocking, she felt a needle-stab on the underside of her left foot. A sharp pebble? Not that. It couldn't be. It was different. Strange. She moved further out and gave a shout of encouragement to Emily, who was doing well. The fearless Simon was up on his board again and again and had one particularly long run-in that was truly impressive.

There was no doubt Rick was enjoying himself, and so were the Buckley parents. She couldn't always see them now, or Simon and Emily because of the intervening bodies, but it was obvious that things were going well.

She was increasingly aware that her

foot was even more painful now. In fact it hurt too much for her to get up on her board. Something was definitely wrong. She lay face-down and waited for the next wave to carry her into shore and then stood up on one foot so she could take a look at the other.

Her foot was badly swollen. She hobbled out of the water. Then she looked at it again. What could have caused it to balloon up at such a rate? Seriously concerned now, she tried putting some weight on it but gasped in agony.

Among all the activity she couldn't see Rick or the others. For a dizzying moment she couldn't see anything else either. Then the swirling mist cleared and she knew she would have to manage alone. Hopping and leaning on her board as a support, she started on the long trek up the beach. She took frequent rests, breathing hard in the vain hope of lessening the pain.

'Harriet!'

She heard the call but didn't see Jem at first. Then she looked up in disbelief as he reached her.

'Harriet, what's wrong?'

He gave a low whistle as she lifted her foot for him to see.

'When did this happen?'

'Just now. A little while ago. I don't know. I . . . '

He took her board from her. 'Here, lean on me.'

She felt decidedly woozy again now and was glad of his support. He was wearing shorts and a white T-shirt and through it his body fclt warm. He put his arm round her. 'Come on, Harriet. As quick as you can. We need to get up to the lifeguards' hut. Can you manage that?'

She could, with his help, but it still seemed a long way.

'It looks very much as if you've been bitten by a weeverfish,' he said. 'Horrible things lurking beneath the sand. It happened to me once. The pain's excruciating.'

She bit her lip, concentrating hard. Several people were sitting outside the hut in a circle, each with one foot in a bowl.

'Hot water,' said Jem. 'It breaks down the poison if it's done within ten minutes.'

A seat was found for her and a bowl of hot water produced. She put her foot in gingerly.

'All right, Harriet?' said Jem.

She nodded, relieved that something was happening and that Jem was here with her. Glad, too, that she didn't have to move anywhere else until the pain lessened and the swelling went down.

But it didn't seem to be working. After a while Jem looked at his watch. 'No better?'

Two of her fellow suffers were getting up to go now. More hot water was brought to top up her bowl.

'It looks as if we're too late for this treatment,' the lifeguard said. He looked regretful. 'More than ten minutes must have passed since it happened. You'll need medical attention. Sorry. We can't help there, I'm afraid. I'll phone through to the medical centre and tell them you're on your way. A duty doctor will be there to meet you.'

'Thank you,' said Jem. 'My car's nearby. I'll get her there.'

Harriet felt so unwell it seemed like a bad dream, and it wasn't until she was in Jem's Land Rover and they were on their way that she thought of Rick, who was unaware of what had happened.

'Rick's going to think I've got myself drowned,' she said in dismay.

'He wasn't keeping an eye on you?'

'Why should he? He was concentrating on other people. He doesn't know.'

Jem showed no reaction and she thought he didn't care. But he pulled into the next layby and got out his mobile phone. 'Dawna?' he said.

Relieved, Harriet sank back in her seat and closed her eyes. Dawna would sort it out. Jem hadn't told her why his cousin wasn't down on the beach with him, but she had full confidence that she would get the message to Rick somehow.

# 11

Jem made sure Harriet took the first dose of prescribed antibiotics immediately. Still feeling slightly nauseous, she did as she was told and then was glad to be seated in his vehicle on their way back to Roslarren.

'Feeling any better now?' he asked.

She shook her head.

'Give it time. The antibiotics will work, you'll see.'

'But how long . . . ?'

'Just rest and recover from the shock, Harriet. That's all you need to do for the moment.'

'But I can't rest,' she said hopelessly.

He said nothing more and in his silence she seemed to detect censure of Rick and all he expected of her. But it wasn't like that, she wanted to cry out. It was her choice to come down to Roslarren and help him, and she couldn't let him down now. There was no meal to prepare for clients this evening, and since she wasn't hungry maybe Rick would agree to eat out. But what if bookings for the complete package suddenly took off? How could she cope then?

They reached the outskirts of the village and Jem drove slowly down the steep hill and up again on the other side and through the open gates of Roslarren House. When he drew up outside the front door he sat for a moment looking up at the building that seemed to be slumbering in the afternoon sunshine.

'A fine position,' he murmured. Then he sprang out and came round to her side to open the door.

For a moment she didn't move. 'But what's happened to my board?' she said. 'I've only just thought . . .'

'Don't worry about that. It's safe in the lifeguard's hut. They'll look after it. Let me have a look at your foot.'

She held it out for him to see.

'Mmn. Nothing doing yet. I'll help

you inside. I think a hot drink's in order, don't you? I can see to that too.'

He helped her out and she balanced on one foot with the sunshine beaming down on her. The noise from the beach down below seemed to come up and hit her, and it was a relief to get inside the cool house. She sat at the kitchen table, her foot up on another chair. Jem appeared to know instinctively where everything was and set about the job with quiet efficiency.

'Tea, coffee?' he asked.

'Tea, please.'

'Tea coming up.'

She drank her tea scalding hot, and when she had finished he gazed at her intently.

'You look more human now,' he said, smiling.

Seeing him sitting there with his cup of tea before him, she felt reassured that everything wasn't as bad as she had feared. For the first time she thought of Jem's ruined afternoon. 'I'm so sorry,' she said.

'For what? That you trod on the weeverfish deliberately?'

She shuddered. 'I didn't know weeverfish existed. I'd heard of sea urchins and jellyfish but not weeverfish.'

'They're not common, thankfully. They lurk just beneath the sand, ready to strike their prey with their needle-sharp spines.'

'It was such a surprise. I didn't know what it was. It was frightening.'

'From the jolly party of sufferers at the lifeguard's hut it seems there's an invasion of weeverfish at the moment,' Jem said. 'It happens sometimes after especially warm weather. Dawna would tell you to warn your clients to wear something on their feet at all times. But then it's good for her business, isn't it?'

'We'll get her to bring some here to have ready for sale.'

'Good thinking.'

It was about all the thinking she was capable of at the moment. But she was aware that she should be thanking Jem for all he had done for her this afternoon. He had been invaluable, not only for the practical help he had provided but also for the moral support his presence gave her. But somehow she had difficulty framing the words. She yawned, wishing she had the energy to get out of her wetsuit and find some suitable footwear for one foot.

As Jem got up to offer more tea they heard the front door burst open, and the next moment Rick appeared in the kitchen doorway, glaring at them with a reddened face. 'What's the meaning of this?'

Jem, about to open the packet of tea bags, looked surprised. 'Didn't Dawna tell you?'

'Tell me what? I haven't seen Dawna. All I knew was that Harriet had gone. No sign of her. What was I to think? And now I find you up here socialising with no thought of anyone else.'

'Not socialising . . . '

'Yep, that's what it looks like. What happened to our arrangement for letting each other know we've left the sea, Harriet? No surfboard left as a signal, no . . . '

'Stop it, Rick,' she cried.

'What sort of example is it messing about here when no one had seen you for ages?'

Jem stepped forward. 'That's enough.'

'Enough, is it?' The next moment his fist shot out and caught Jem on the side of his face.

Shocked, Harriet leapt up. The chair where her swollen foot had rested crashed to the floor.

Seeing what he had done, Rick leaned back against the wall and stared at Jem. 'I'm sorry. I . . . '

Jem's left hand was clapped to his cheek. He made no attempt to retaliate. 'I think I should leave,' he said quietly.

The deep silence when he had gone was electric. Then Harriet righted the chair and leaned on it. Any feeling of weakness had gone now. She glared at Rick. 'Jem phoned Dawna,' she said. 'She promised to tell you what happened.'

'And what *did* happen?'

'She didn't tell you?'

'She wasn't there.'

'But didn't you see my board at the lifeguard's hut? Didn't they tell you . . . ?'

'What?' he spat out.

'I trod on a weeverfish. It was agony. I wasn't the only one. Jem was there. He had to take me to the medical centre. He phoned Dawna.'

'I didn't know,' Rick said. His fury left him suddenly. He pulled out another chair and sank down at the table. Harriet held out her swollen foot for him to see.

'It's bad?'

'At the moment. I'm on antibiotics. Jem said they'd work soon.'

'Jem,' he groaned. 'Oh, what have I done?'

\* \* \*

Harriet couldn't believe how difficult it was dragging herself on one bare foot up the uncarpeted stairs to her room. Determined to do it on her own, she had spurned Rick's offer of help. Wetsuits weren't easy to peel off at the best of times, but at last she managed to ease it off and left it in a heap on the floor. Luckily her clothes were handy and her shorts and yellow T-shirt were easy to get on, but even so, the effort exhausted her and she was glad to lie down on the bed for a moment.

How long she slept she didn't know, but when at last she stirred and opened her eyes she was aware that the sun no longer shone directly into her room.

At once the recent events flooded her mind and she felt again the chill that filled her as Rick's hand met its target. She heard the crash of her falling chair and her own gasp of horror. It was as if there was no hope for them now in Breaking Waves because of what Rick had done. She had seen the utter hopelessness in his face when Jem left and knew that once discouraged, Rick found it hard to regain his equilibrium.

She struggled up to a sitting position and leaned back against the wall trying to make sense of it all. Through Dawna, Rick would know of Jem's initial interest in the property. But why should that make any difference between them? Roslarren House was Rick's inheritance, and local approval for the setting up of the surf school had been encouraging.

She was certain she hadn't imagined Jem's barely disguised disapproval of Rick or his continual interest in Roslarren House. Had Rick picked up on this, too, and resented it? And was that why he had been so quick to jump to the wrong conclusions? Jem had looked really shocked, and no wonder. Rick's attack on him was totally out of order.

She owed Jem a huge debt, but she owed Rick's family one too. His parents had taken her into their home when she had needed support and she would never forget that. Now, when Rick's father was unwell and anxious about his son, she had the means to repay that debt. Her loyalty must be to Rick, who would be deeply regretting his hasty action and finding it hard to go on.

# 12

She looked at the clock on her bedside table. Six o'clock! Suddenly she felt hungry and a lot better after her sleep. She should be attending to Rick, suggesting he should order a takeaway, checking that he was all right. Reaching for one of her trainers at the side of her bed, she put it on. Her swollen foot would have to make do with a flip-flop.

Somehow she got herself to the top of the stairs and, leaning hard on the banister, thumped her way down.

The kitchen door swung open and Dawna stood on the threshold. Her face lit up on seeing her. 'You're awake! I looked in on you just now and you were well away.'

'Have you seen Rick?'

'No sign of him. Down in the sea again, I shouldn't wonder. But what about you? Such bad luck with the weeverfish. Is it still painful?'

'A bit.'

'A lot by the look of it. Here, let me help you.' She assisted Harriet into a chair by the kitchen table and then sat down herself and looked at her in concern.

Harriet shrugged as she reached for the biscuit tin on the shelf behind her and took three biscuits. 'Jem was brilliant,' she said. 'I don't know what I'd have done without him. How is he? Did Rick hurt him badly?'

'Rick? What do you mean?'

'Jem didn't tell you about Rick lashing out at him?'

'Rick did *what*?'

'He's really sorry, Dawna. He hit Jem hard in the face. He didn't know I'd left the beach, you see. He had no idea where I was. And then when he saw Jem and me here together after he'd brought me back, it was too much for him.'

Dawna stared at Harriet, aghast. 'Rick didn't see the note I left?'

'Where was it?'

'On your notice board on the beach, firmly attached. I had to do that. My friend had an emergency and I was helping out with her youngster. That's why I wasn't down at the beach with Jem. I rushed down quickly with the note when he phoned. It seemed to best thing to do.'

'And Rick should have seen it.'

'But he didn't.'

'Could it have blown off?'

Dawna frowned. 'I don't think so.' She looked at the biscuits forgotten in Harriet's hand. 'Are you hungry?'

'I haven't eaten for hours.'

'Then let me do something about it.' She got up and rummaged in the fridge. 'Ham and eggs do you?'

'Please. And you too?'

Harriet ate the biscuits and then took two more. By this time Dawna had the eggs in the frying pan and was laying the table with knives and forks. She found a loaf of bread in the bin and tomatoes in the fridge. It made an excellent and quick meal for the two of them. Afterwards they stayed sitting at the table, going over and over again the mystery of the missing note.

'Poor Rick,' Dawna said at last. 'He'll be devastated at what he's done when there was no reason. Who'd be keen to book in for surf lessons if it got about? Thank goodness there were no witnesses.'

'Except me,' said Harriet. She thought of Jem and wondered where he was now. It was hard to think of him hurt by someone close to her. Prospective clients might not be the only ones put off coming to Breaking Waves.

'Ah well, there's no real harm done,' Dawna said at last.

'Only to Jem.'

'Don't look like that. He'll get over it.'

Physically perhaps, Harriet reflected. She thought of the expression on his face as he said it was best he should go. She might not even see him again. He lived near Fraddon, some miles from Roslarren. And he wasn't likely to be booking in for a surfing lesson here after this.

Dawna scraped her chair back as she

got up. She smiled at Harriet. 'I'll make you another coffee and then I'll go down to the beach and find Rick. See what he's got to say for himself. I won't be too hard on him, I promise.'

After she had gone clattering out, Harriet leaned forward in her chair and examined her foot, willing the swelling to have gone down a little. She prodded it gently. Maybe it had, just a bit. But maybe it hadn't. She wasn't going to be any use to Rick in this condition. It was fortunate they had no more bookings for surfing lessons for the next few days. She certainly wouldn't be able to oversee any beginners. She wouldn't be able to do much else either.

She picked up the local paper Dawna had left but she couldn't concentrate on it for long. With no bookings for the next few days Rick would have time to sort out some of the buildings at the back of the house once used to store fishing tackle and boat-building materials by previous owners. He had told her that the space out there could be useful in many ways apart from storage. He hadn't specified what they could be used for and she suspected that he didn't really know himself. But he had been full of all sorts of plans and ideas. She hoped he still was.

She turned the pages desultorily until her attention was caught by a headline that interested her:

## WEEVERFISH ATTACK ON SURFERS AT ROSLARREN

With dismay she read the sensational account of the little fish whose spines were toxic and caused such excruciating pain. This was bad publicity for the place and especially for Breaking Waves. Anyone putting Roslarren into Google would read of this.

She went through it several times, thinking hard. Maybe Rick shouldn't be attending to the outhouses but should be down on the beach at all times, showing by example that there was nothing to fear if you wore suitable footwear when in the water. Good publicity was what was needed now.

And a website for Breaking Waves.

Steven had promised to set it up for them. He seemed confident that it would promote more takers. So what was the problem with the finance? Maybe he wouldn't be in too much of a hurry to be reimbursed? It was an offer too good to miss, especially as she would have time during the next few days to gather all the information and photos they needed and send them to him. Some of Rick's filming of lessons would be good too.

Before she could change her mind she pulled out her mobile she kept handy in the pocket of her shorts. On it she had put Steven's home number. She clicked on it now.

★　★　★

As Jem had promised, the antibiotics began to kick in and by Monday morning the pain in Harriet's foot had eased considerably. She even managed to get her sandals on both feet, although the straps on the still slightly swollen foot wouldn't quite do up. She hoped this would change during the day.

Rick, much subdued at breakfast, looked at her warily. 'The surf's good today,' he said.

'See you later, then,' she said in answer to his unspoken question. 'I'll be busy up here at the house.'

Yesterday evening, suitably chastened, he sent an email of apology to Jem but as yet had had no reply. The thought crossed her mind that Jem might contact him today. She would like to see his name come up on Rick's email and know that he had been in touch.

She didn't tell Rick that she had already been in contact with Steven and he had told her what she needed to do to aid him in setting up the website. The anticipation of starting work on it was great and she couldn't wait to begin. She understood, of course, that he couldn't set about it until this evening after work.

She sat down at the laptop and began. Engrossed, she almost missed hearing the house phone ring, but its insistent tone alerted her at last.

'Is that the surf school?' a female voice demanded.

'Breaking Waves. How can I help you?'

'He said to ring you. We're down on the beach, just arrived. Can you book us in?'

Fortunately the booking ledger was handy and she flipped it open and picked up a pen. The booking was for five people, all girls, wanting a single lesson next day.

'Have you surfed before?' Harriet asked, busily writing.

'Not so you'd notice. Beginners all. Is that a problem?'

'Of course not,' she hastened to assure them. 'I look forward to meeting you.'

Another booking. That was good even though it was for one lesson only.

The phone rang again.

'Hello?'

Jem's deep voice took her by surprise. 'How are you, Harriet? How's the foot?'

For some reason tears sprang to her eyes. This was stupid. She took a deep breath. 'Jem! It's good to hear from you. Are you all right?'

'Why shouldn't I be? I'm used to that sort of thing — people hitting me about, pushing me into bogs, hurling me over cliffs.'

'If you say so.' She gave a shaky laugh.

'But what about you, Harriet?'

'The swelling's going down now and it's not half as painful. I've just taken another booking so things are looking up.'

'He's keeping you hard at it then?'

'And why not?' she said with spirit. 'That's what I'm here for.'

He laughed. 'But not all the time, surely?'

'I have to earn my keep.'

'You seem to be doing that and more. But don't waste your energies on something that might not be worthwhile in the long run. You're worth more than that, Harriet.'

She was silenced by his assumption. There it was again, more in the open now, and she didn't know how to answer him. He had done so much for her, and she was grateful, but there was always this suspicion of watchfulness on his part, of censure for what they were trying to do at Breaking Waves.

'Harriet, are you still there?'

'I haven't thanked you properly, Jem,' she said. 'I haven't said how much I appreciate the help you gave me.'

'Think nothing of it. I was there and that was good. I'm glad you're on the mend. Look after yourself.'

Harriet put the phone down and stood leaning on the wall, deep in thought. Hearing Jem's voice had disturbed her and had interrupted her enthusiasm for amassing information for the website. All she wanted to do now was lie down on her bed and sleep. She returned to the dining room, sat down and stared lethargically at the blank screen of the laptop. It seemed to be telling her something so that she no longer had the energy to get her work back into view. A button to press, that was all, but she couldn't do it.

Moments later when she heard sounds of Rick's return, she turned around in her seat and waited for him to find her. He came in barefoot but still in his wetsuit. He seemed to bring in with him the feel of the wind and the waves, and the smell of salty seaweed.

'Guess what, Harriet,' he said, his face shining with enthusiasm. 'Six more want to take lessons. Tomorrow afternoon. Intermediates, most of them. One is more advanced and wants to perfect his style. That's what he said. Good, isn't it?'

She looked at him in dismay. 'Didn't you know that five beginners will be there too?'

'Of course. I got them to phone you, didn't I? They didn't seem to know what's what and I thought you could put them straight.'

'It's you that needs putting straight,' she said. 'A group of eleven people, all abilities, and me like this unable to help. What are you thinking of, Rick?'

'No problem. You'll be okay by tomorrow.'

'Rick, listen to me. Please be sensible. Whether I'm better or not, it makes sense to have a beginners' session only in the morning and the more advanced separately, in the afternoon. Have you got their details? Why don't you phone them and rearrange?'

Rick shrugged and turned away. The bright atmosphere seemed to dim and she looked at him in despair.

'Need I ask? You haven't got a contact number?'

'I'll manage.'

She had no doubt he would after a fashion, but he wouldn't be able to give of his best. But nothing she could say would make him change his mind, and in the end she gave up.

Dawna joined in, too, when she brought round a pizza she'd made for their evening meal. But Rick was adamant that he could cope, and it seemed he could, because he was cheerful on Tuesday evening saying how well it had all gone. He had collected pasties for himself and Harriet and they ate them in companionable silence at the kitchen table in the early evening.

'I'm off out later,' Rick said when he got up to get some ice-cream out of the freezer when they had finished.

'Anywhere exciting?'

'You don't mind?'

'Why should I?'

'How's your foot now?'

'Better,' she said, holding it up for him to see.

'Pity we've got no bookings for tomorrow.'

He sounded offhand and that was surprising. She wondered if he had made other plans but wouldn't ask. Relations between them hadn't been as good as she would like these last couple of days. A host of bookings might alter that. Maybe the website would see to it.

'I'll have an early night,' she said.

# 13

During the days that followed Rick was down on the beach as often as he could manage, to make the most of the spell of warm dry weather and good surfing conditions. Once or twice he got a booking for a lesson and came up to the house looking pleased with himself. By Thursday Harriet had completely recovered the use of her foot and was happy to take a trip to the supermarket. Fully active again, she had made sure the bedrooms were all ready for occupation and the bathrooms stocked with clean towels and toiletries.

All that was needed now were some firm bookings for the accommodation. Unfortunately they were slow in coming.

She cooked *coq au vin* for their evening meal, Rick's favourite. As they sat down to it she noticed that he kept looking warily at her, as if he was anxious about something.

'Rick?' she said.

He picked up his knife and fork. 'Would you say you were overworked, Harriet?'

'Hardly.' She smiled.

'You haven't had a day off since you got here.'

'What's brought this on?'

He shrugged and reached for his water glass. Looking at it critically, he put it down again. 'I was going to ask you if you'd like to take a day off. Everyone should have one. Yep, I should have thought of it before.'

She was touched. Things hadn't been easy for him lately. A few bills had come in and he'd had a difficult meeting at the bank. Once he'd gone off for the afternoon without saying where he was going and returned subdued with none of the noisy clatter that was usual.

'That's good of you, Rick,' she said. 'Did Dawna suggest it? I haven't seen her since she brought the pizza. I hope she's all right.' She had considered ringing her friend, but then thought she might be extra busy and it would be best to do it later — only to forget until it was too late at night and Dawna would be sure to have gone to bed. 'I'll phone as soon as we finish eating.'

'Nope, not Dawna. If you must know, I went to see her cousin at his place near Fraddon. I found him sorting out his gear at the back.'

Surprised, Harriet looked at him, a forkful of chicken halfway to her mouth. 'You actually went to see Jem?'

'Yep, that's what I said.'

'To apologise in person?'

'I thought he might be expecting another blow on the face when he saw me but he seemed all right about it. We got talking about diving. He used to do a lot at one time. Mostly off the Welsh coast when he was at university. Did you know that? He's a decent guy when you get to know him.'

Harriet took a deep breath of relief. She had hated the signs of disagreement between the two of them and had been shocked when it came to a head in such an aggressive way. It was brave of Rick to make that journey.

'That's great, Rick. I'm really pleased.'

'He might be over this way sometime.'

A warm glow rippled through her. She had thought she might not see him again. But now, it seemed, everything was back to normal. She really would phone Dawna this evening.

But there was no need. As soon as they had finished eating, Dawna came bursting in full of plans for a party the following evening. 'At my place,' she said. 'Nothing for you to do, Harriet. It's all arranged. We'll be barbecuing, weather permitting. If not, we can all crowd indoors. I thought we'd celebrate your recovery.'

'It was only a weeverfish sting,' Harriet said, laughing.

Dawna laughed too. 'Any excuse.'

'Sit down and have some coffee and tell me why you haven't been in touch.'

'I told you. Arranging the barbecue.

Inviting people.'

'Who in particular?'

'Friends, clients of mine. Anyone who might spread the word about Breaking Waves.'

Jem too? It was more than likely, Harriet thought.

'Do you need any of our equipment?' Rick asked.

'An extra barbecue would be good, thanks. We can do with two. I've plenty of charcoal.'

'How many people are we talking about?'

'Not sure, but it doesn't matter.'

'So you've been busy,' said Harriet. She carried three mugs of coffee to the table and opened the biscuit tin. Dawna took one and consumed it in one go.

'You've eaten?' Harriet asked.

'No time.'

'Then it's lucky I made too much for us. The rest is in the slow cooker. I'll get it.'

'Typical,' said Rick. 'Ignore us for days and then come round here to eat us out of house and home.'

Dawna helped herself to a knife and fork from the drawer and sat down again. 'Bring it on, Harriet. It smells good.'

When she had finished and the kitchen had been cleared, they went into the dining room for Rick to show Dawna the videos he had made of his surfing lessons. After a while Harriet left them to it, pleading fatigue. She wanted some time on her own to relish her contentment that everything was back to how it had been when Rick's enthusiasm and delight in Breaking Waves was at its height. Only good could come of the effort Dawna was putting in for them. She couldn't wait for the following evening to be here.

* * *

Dawna's small terrace house at the end of a long row was on the outskirts of Roslarren. Behind it her long garden stretched to fields and slightly rising ground. A large paved area near the house was perfect for setting up the two barbecues.

She had made a fruit punch in a huge cauldron-like container to get things started. She handed Harriet and Rick a glassful each when they arrived behind a crowd of gaily dressed people.

'Fancy dress?' whispered Rick to Harriet as they joined them on the lawn.

'Of course not. Behave yourself.' She was feeling good in her new skirt and flowered top, glad that it, too, was in bold shades of pink and red.

Two men in shorts and sleeveless T-shirts were busy at the barbecues with a lot of repartee flying back and forth. The smell of braising meat wafted across the garden and made Harriet's eyes water. She didn't know what was in the punch but suspected it wasn't as non-alcoholic as she had been led to believe.

It seemed that Dawna had spared no expense and things were going with a swing. Someone turned up the music so it could be heard above the hum of conversation.

'Come and eat, everybody,' Dawna called at last.

Various salad dishes were displayed on a couple of long tables together with a silver-foiled tray laden with an assortment of cheeses.

'Something for everyone,' said Rick at Harriet's side. 'D'you think it'll pay off for Breaking Waves and we'll get masses of bookings from all this lot?'

'Enquiries, maybe.' Harriet had already noticed the poster advertising their surfing school pinned to a silver birch at one side of the lawn. She had the feeling that her friend would insist that everyone went home eventually clutching one of their leaflets.

Rick left her to go for a closer look at the poster and she saw someone talking to him, hopefully asking about it. Dawna was a good friend doing her best to bring attention to what they had on offer. She glanced across at her now, happy and glowing in her short scarlet dress. Then she noticed that among the throng by the table was another person in red too, slightly shorter than Dawna and with long dark hair.

Harriet stared in disbelief. Chloë, invited to Dawna's party? It seemed highly unlikely.

At that moment Rick noticed her too. 'Chloë, is it really you?' he called out.

She came running across to him at the same time as Dawna turned away from the salad table and noticed what was happening. Her lips tightened and she walked carefully across the intervening space towards them.

And now Rick had his arm round both of them. 'Two lovely girls,' he said, smiling from one to the other.

Helplessly, Harriet watched. She was in the middle of a bad dream and what she did next would have dire consequences. But she could do nothing but stand there and watch the drama unfold in front of her as if her strappy sandals were cemented into the springy grass.

'What are you doing here, Chloë?' Dawna said in a voice like ice.

'I simply couldn't resist it when Tom

told me about it. He invited me to come with him. Said you wouldn't mind. I'll go now if you like.'

'Don't think of it,' said Rick heatedly. 'We don't want her to do that, do we Dawna?'

'Tom?' Dawna said suspiciously.

'My boss. He's a good customer of yours. Always in your shop buying bits and pieces.'

'Oh yes, Tom.'

'He's here somewhere. Shall I get him to vouch for me?'

Before Dawna could reply, there was a commotion over by the barbecue and she went to sort it out. Harriet followed her.

'We can't have run out of veggie burgers already,' Dawna said in dismay. 'I got packets of them.'

'Here they are,' one of the cooks proclaimed, fishing out a box of them from beneath the table. 'Someone hid them on purpose and I've a good idea who.'

His fellow cook grinned. 'I've been sussed.'

Dawna shrugged. 'Those two!' She didn't

mention Chloë and Harriet didn't either, but Dawna's bright look had faded. It was too bad Chloë turning up like that when she wasn't invited. Rick's obvious delight didn't help matters either. Harriet turned her back on them both and saw Jem coming across the grass. Here was a guest Dawna was delighted to see.

'Hey,' he said, extricating himself from the huge hug she gave him. 'Sorry I'm late. What can I do now that I'm here?'

'Look after Harriet,' Dawna said promptly.

'Since when have I needed looking after?' said Harriet.

'I can think of one occasion.'

'Well, yes, that.' She smiled at him. He looked bronzed and healthy in his white shirt and chinos.

'Dawna!' someone called. 'We need you over here.'

'Grab yourselves some food, you two,' she called back over her shoulder as she went off.

'Then we'd better do as we're told,' Jem said, smiling.

# 14

With their plates piled high, they walked to the end of the garden, the scent from a white lilac bush wafting towards them.

'I need to sit down somewhere to eat,' Jem said. 'I've been on my feet all day. And I daresay you have too, now that you appear to be in the land of the living once more.'

'You could say that.'

'Busy at Breaking Waves?'

'Not so you'd notice.'

'Your website looks good.'

She smiled, flattered that he had troubled to look. But was he just checking up on them?

Dawna had placed garden chairs wherever she could and here near the fence at the end of the garden, they had been ignored. Jem put his plate down on one of them.

'Drinks,' he said. 'Stay here on guard

if you will, Harriet, and I'll organise some.'

Harriet sat with her plate in her lap, listening to the muted party noise going on behind her. The smell of crushed grass was pleasant and the cooling evening air was soothing on her face. Even the thought of Chloë doing her usual monopolising-Rick act failed to disturb the beauty of the moment.

Jem was soon back, and as they ate he talked of his work and how he was leading a field trip on Sunday in his programme for conserving Cornwall's geological heritage.

'That sounds rather grand,' said Harriet.

'It's a good day out for the knowledge-able, and for the not-so-knowledgeable too. There's something for everyone and a great deal to see, but it needs an especially low tide to do the complete walk. We won't quite have that, but no matter. I promise it'll be worthwhile.'

'I think you've mentioned the low tide before. Or Dawna has.'

'Sorry. I'm becoming a geological bore. And there I was, thinking I was interesting you, and all the time you were just being polite.'

She smiled at him. 'I'm never polite.'

'Not like your good friend Rick then.'

'He's not always my good friend. My frustrating friend. I'm supposed to be here in Roslarren helping to make Breaking Waves a success, but it's not always easy working with him.'

'But you do care for him?'

'I've cared for his family over the years but now there's only his father left. I'm doing it for him really. I owe him a big debt.'

He looked at her enquiringly. 'You do?'

'Rick's parents stepped in and helped when I needed them. I like to think they saved my reason.'

'Then there's nothing between you and Rick? In a special way, I mean?'

She shook her head, feeling warmth from his interest seep into her. 'He feels like my brother.'

'Then why do you take it all so much

to heart, if you don't mind my asking?'

'For his father's sake. I owe a big obligation to his family for taking me in when I was young. My parents died, you see — one after the other, with a few weeks in between. His parents were wonderful. And his father, a widower now, is very frail. His deep worry about his son is making him ill, though I think there may be something seriously wrong anyway that he's not telling anyone about. So here I am, trying to help, but not being very successful at it.'

She had never gone into such detail before to anyone, but there was something about Jem's sympathetic interest that brought it all out. She found herself telling him of the promotion she had turned down and how she hadn't minded about it a bit because of this chance to show her gratitude for what the Seton family had done for her.

'Dawna told me about you being deputy manager of a restaurant, so you must have some idea of running a business,' Jem said.

'I like to think so.'

Jem bit into a piece of chicken and then ate the remains of his salad in silence. Harriet, too, was thoughtful. The peace she had enjoyed for such a brief moment had faded away because of her anxieties about Breaking Waves that lay all the time beneath the surface of her mind.

'It's a good field trip I'm leading tomorrow,' he said suddenly. 'One of my favourite geological trails.'

She smiled, pleased he had changed the subject and lightened the atmosphere. 'It's somewhere up near Tintagel, isn't it?'

'Trebarwith Strand.'

'Not far from Padstow?'

'That's it.'

'It sounds really interesting.'

'I'm sure you'd enjoy it, Harriet. Would you like to come with us as my guest?'

'It's an appealing idea.'

'More than an idea. A plan. A definite one, yes? You have walking

162

shoes, stout ones?'

She smiled and glanced at her feet. Then she lifted the left one, now back to its usual size, and looked at it appreciatively. 'You can't think how good it is to get into these sandals this evening. But, yes, you'll find me suitably booted and clad. And I'll be glad to come, Jem. Rick wants me to have a day off.'

He gave a brief smile. 'I'll pick you up about nine.'

'Perfect.' Harriet yawned and then tried to disguise it. 'Sorry, so much has been happening.'

Her seesawing emotions had been working overtime since Dawna had talked of her party, and it was getting late now. Already dusk had obliterated the trees on the low hill in the distance.

Chloë was nowhere to be seen as they joined the others, but Harriet saw Rick and Dawna holding forth on something obviously engrossing. Breaking Waves? She hoped so.

Dawna had strung up a line of lights

on the cherry trees at the end of the house and to Harriet they looked magical. She felt Jem come close. He tilted her face up to his and she saw the reflection of a thousand colours in his eyes.

'Harriet,' he murmured.

She waited breathlessly for his kiss but it didn't come. Instead a figure in a red dress came running to them.

'You're needed over here,' she cried.

The moment was broken.

'It's Chloë, the girl causing us trouble at Breaking Waves,' said Harriet. 'What does she want now?'

'We'd better find out.'

They joined the crowd near the barbecues. Chloë had pulled a chair forward and someone had helped her up on it. From a standing position she looked impressive and there were murmurs of approval.

'Just to say, everyone, that there are magnificent desserts laid out indoors and Rick's going to be dishing them out. Isn't that right, Rick? Lead on, then, Rick!' She jumped off the chair and came to take his arm.

In the dimming light he looked bemused. Harriet didn't look at Dawna but she knew what her reaction would be: total incomprehension mixed with exasperation.

★ ★ ★

Harriet was ready and waiting outside Roslarren House in good time next morning. Jem, early, was pleased to see her there. He jumped down from his vehicle.

'All set then? I'll take your rucksack and put it in the back.'

She handed it to him and her jacket as well. Her jeans were her oldest, most comfortable ones, but the blue T-shirt beneath her sweater was new, a change from the yellow Breaking Waves one.

The morning was calm, the sun threatening to emerge from its blanket of wispy cloud and flood the beach at any moment. In the distance the surf looked good. Around her she smelt the scent from an early rose climbing over the fence, and a feeling of deep happiness stole over her.

Jem smiled at her as they set off. 'I see you're well shod today.'

'I've got a change of footwear for afterwards in my rucksack,' she said. 'And my packed lunch.'

'We can get coffee and tea somewhere easily enough,' he said as he put the vehicle into gear and they set off. 'On a day like this I suspect that most of us will have brought our food with us. Nothing like eating in the open air among a group of like-minded people.'

They parked some time later at the designated car park. Three cars were already there and the occupants, standing close by, eyed them expectantly.

'Some of our group, I think,' Jem said. He produced a clipboard, ready to tick off names as he greeted them.

Harriet stood a little to one side and watched the proceedings as others arrived and made themselves known. She saw that the group was made up of all ages from about seventeen to middle age or even older. She wondered how many had done this kind of thing before and were keen geoconservationists. They set off to walk down to the beach. One of them looked bemused as Jem suggested that they should take particular note of the overhang at the base of the cliff where they would see pale and fine-grained rock.

'This is banded slates with limestones of the Barras Nose Formation. It's Lower Carboniferous in age, of course,' he told them.

'Of course,' muttered a voice at Harriet's side. 'Simply fascinating.'

It was obvious from her tone that she thought the opposite and Harriet took a quick interested look at her.

'I'm Erica,' her companion said. 'And you?'

'Harriet.'

In her black leggings, red jacket and brown woolly hat, Erica resembled a discontented robin.

'So you're not yet totally convinced that you're in for an interesting time?' Harriet said, smiling.

Erica gave a hollow laugh. 'I can't be doing with all this rocky, shingly stuff. Give me a soft sandy beach any day and then I'm happy. It's Lyndon, my husband, who's into this sort of thing. Just look at him now. Full of it.'

A tall, thin man with an intelligent-looking face was deep in conversation with Jem. Erica glanced at him and her voice softened. 'He's simply obsessed with all this nonsense, so I have to come along to keep an eye on him. No sense of direction at all, poor man. He could so easily end up in Wales on the way back. I'm not joking. Someone has to look after him.'

They were almost on the beach now and Jem broke off his conversation to gather the group round him.

'Note the squashed lava bombs in the smooth rocks at your feet,' he said. 'And now before we go on the beach and follow the cliffs along to the right, we'll take a look at the stream. See how the water has eroded the soft rocks to smooth potholes. If the sand level is low enough you can sometimes see an arch over its lower end.'

'Miraculous,' Erica breathed.

Harriet bit back a giggle as Jem invited them to look at the high cliff face beyond, where several fault lines ran steeply down and the sea had gradually eroded the weaker rock at the bottom so that a cave had formed.

They moved now along the beach near the cliffs to the right, lingering every now and again for Jem to draw their attention to points of great interest to everyone except Erica, who kept up a low-pitched monologue Harriet found hard to ignore because it was so entertaining.

'You don't mean to say you are interested in all this, Harriet?' Erica said in disbelief as they reached Vean Hole and moved on to the point at which they would soon be turning back.

'Well yes, I am,' Harriet admitted.

'I don't understand half of it, though. I wish I didn't feel so ignorant.' She looked around at the other members of the party. They all looked interested enough to make Jem's job as leader worthwhile. Erica's husband, Lyndon, seemed entranced by it all and was standing gazing up at the cliffs with a rapt expression on his face.

'It's not safe to go much further with this state of the tide,' Jem said. 'We could easily get cut off. But just along here you can look right up into Lanterdan Slate Quarry. Once it was the biggest in north Cornwall for quarrying Upper Delabole slate. The wharf has long gone, courtesy of the sea.'

There was still much to see, but most people opted to sit down and eat their packed lunches. Lyndon, though, was obviously on too much of a high to want that.

'Take no notice of the silly man,' said Erica, patting a rock at her side for Harriet to make use of as a seat. 'I'll feed him when we get back to the car.'

While they were eating, Jem made a point of joining each small group in turn to check that everyone was happy with the geological trail and the information he had given them. Harriet watched him surreptitiously, impressed with the way he was interested and concerned with what each of them was telling him, even Erica.

He had left the pair of them until last and only then did he unwrap his packet of sandwiches. 'Your husband has been telling me of your self-sacrifice in coming with him today, Erica,' he said. 'I hope it's not been too much of a strain?'

'Not at all,' said Erica brightly. 'Harriet has kept me well entertained.'

Harriet nearly swallowed a piece of cheese the wrong way. 'D'you really think so?' she said, her eyes watering.

Jem threw her an amused look. 'Erica has been with us before,' he said.

Erica smiled. 'And I'm so pleased to meet Harriet again.'

'Again?' said Harriet, perplexed.

Jem laughed as he stood up and went to join Lyndon.

A few moments passed before the penny dropped, and then Harriet moved uncomfortably on her rock seat. 'I felt such a fool falling at his feet like that,' she said.

'Romantic,' Erica suggested.

'Not a bit of it.'

'You're here today, aren't you? Enough said.'

Whatever she said would make matters worse, Harriet thought. Best to ignore it. 'All that volcanic stuff Jem told us back there,' she said. 'Don't you find it incredible?'

'I'd like to find some of that fool's gold,' Erica said dreamily.

'Great big crystals of gold pyrite contained in the fine-grained tuffs of the volcanic rock,' Harriet agreed. 'I think that's what he said.'

Erica sat up straight. 'How big?'

'Five millimetres.'

'*That* big? Wow and double wow! But how big is that really?'

Smiling, Harriet indicated with her forefinger and thumb.

'Almost nothing,' Erica said, disappointed.

When it was time to go, Erica fell back to chivvy her husband along and Harriet felt a little twist of happiness when Jem came to walk beside her. He talked of the pleasure the group today had given him in their genuine interest. 'I only wish I had a suitable headquarters of my own, big enough to hold talks and follow-ups of these geological trail days,' he said.

Harriet could understand the value of that but she didn't like the way this appeared to be going.

'I'd like to hold residential courses too, but of course it's the old question of finance and a suitable property coming on the market. Ah well, one of these fine days, who knows?'

He sounded so sad that she was touched. Dawna had told her how hard he worked for something he had believed in since he was a young boy growing up in a remote place on Bodmin Moor.

The day that had started so well had now begun to cloud over. The sea, still smooth, was now a greyish-blue with a line of rippling foam teasing the rocky shoreline.

'The tide's coming in now,' Jem said. 'We've had the best of the day.'

'It's been a good one,' she said.

'You've enjoyed it?'

'I need to learn more, to read about it and do some research on the internet.'

He smiled. The sun had caught his forehead and as he pushed back a lock of hair she saw the white of his hairline. For a moment he looked vulnerable and she wanted to assure him of her appreciation of the value of what he was doing.

But there could be no doubt of that from the expressions of appreciation from the others he received when they reached the car park and people were preparing to leave.

# 15

They stopped for coffee and huge slabs of saffron cake at a place Jem knew near Delabole. This was a small family-run establishment that specialised in all things Cornish and was tucked away down a narrow lane. It was surprisingly busy and Jem explained that its fame had spread by word of mouth and it now featured in the 'Hidden Cornwall' series of publications. 'So it's no longer a secret,' he said, smiling.

'But it's certainly special.'

They sat outside at a table almost hidden by the overhanging branches of a weeping birch and with the sound of running water nearby. They had almost finished when Harriet's mobile phone rang.

'I'd better answer in case it's something important,' she said.

Rick's voice on the other end sounded

concerned. 'Dad's here,' he said. 'He turned up suddenly ten minutes ago.'

'Where are you?'

'At home, luckily. He wanted to know why I wasn't down on the beach working hard.'

'And did you tell him?'

'I need you here, Harriet. He wants to see you.'

'But how did he get there?'

'He booked himself on a coach tour of Cornwall, can you believe? They're in Newquay tonight. He got a taxi here. He wanted to surprise us.' He had done that only too well, and by the sound of it Rick was in a panic.

'Thanks for warning me,' she said. 'He's your dad, Rick. Entertain him. Show him the videos. Tell him about the barbecues. We've finished the walk now. I'll be back soon.' She glanced at Jem as she replaced the phone in her pocket. 'I'm sorry about that,' she said.

'Me too. It sounds serious.'

'Rick's father has called in unexpectedly.'

'The one who may be seriously ill, who won't admit it but is desperately concerned about Breaking Waves?'

She nodded. 'That's the one.'

'And you're not there to smooth things over, to convince him that all is well and that his son is the world's best businessman?

'Something like that.'

He looked at her sharply. 'Drink up then and we'll be off. You could have a hard job on your hands.'

She let that remark go, more worried than she had led Rick to believe. His father wasn't a fool. He would see for himself that the place was empty except for the two of them. It was hard not to feel that she was letting him down because the surf school wasn't the immediate financial success they had all hoped.

She finished her coffee. Jem didn't seem as disappointed as she was that their time together was coming to an end, so perhaps he wasn't. He had done a good morning's work and would most likely be feeling drained because of it and wanting to get home himself.

Her heart felt like lead as they stood up to leave.

\* \* \*

'Harriet, my dear!' Derek Seton got unsteadily to his feet to greet her.

'Derek, it's good to see you.' She was flushed with pleasure that he was here but was concerned at his appearance, so much frailer than when she had seen him last. It was incredible that he had booked himself in for the coach holiday and was actually here in front of them.

'Rick's been telling me,' he said. 'Weeverfish? Never heard of them.'

She gestured at her walking gear. 'I've been out on a geological trail, looking at cliffs and rocks. I'm fully recovered now.'

They were in the kitchen. She was glad to see that Rick had made a pot of tea and a half-empty plate of biscuits was on the table before them, as well as the used cups and saucers.

Jem had dropped her at the bottom of the drive at her suggestion. He had said little as he got her belongings out for her and she thanked him for her enjoyable day. He had frowned and looked anxious for a moment. 'You'll be all right?'

'Of course,' she had said, surprised at his concern.

She sat down on the empty chair. 'So are you enjoying your venture into Cornwall, Derek?'

'Very much so. They pack a lot in, I must say. The Lost Gardens of Heligan yesterday, the Eden Project today, Land's End and the Lizard tomorrow . . . ' He broke off to cough.

'You make me feel breathless at the thought of all that,' said Harriet, smiling. An arduous programme for someone in Derek's weak state, she thought. 'And so you've missed out on the Eden Project so you could come and see us?'

'It's well worth it, my dear. The Eden Project will still be there next time I come.'

'I hope Rick's been filling you in on what we've been doing here?'

'It's good to see the house again,' he said rather wistfully. 'Such a fine building. Large too. Plenty of room to expand.'

'I'm sorry I wasn't back in time to greet you, Derek,' she said. 'Rick gave me the day off, you see. But now I'm here, let me get you something more substantial to eat.'

'No, my dear. I shall make arrangements to entertain *you*. The evening meal's at six o'clock at the hotel and they say it's in order for you to join us. Unless, of course, you've got things to do here?'

'Nope,' said Rick heartily. 'Sounds good.'

'But I expect you've got a busy week ahead of you?'

'So-so.'

'Have you shown your father our website yet?' said Harriet.

'A website?' Derek said, impressed.

'I'll go and change out of these things,' said Harriet.

When she came down Rick and his father were seated side by side at the table in the dining room with the laptop in front of them. Harriet never tired of accessing their website and she was pleased at Derek's reaction as he viewed the images that came up on screen. This showed progress on their part and gave an optimistic view of the future.

'And people can actually fill in the booking form on their computers?' Derek said in wonder.

A fit of coughing shook him and it was a moment or two before Harriet could reply. She exchanged a quick look with Rick.

'Harriet will show you, Dad,' he said. He stood behind the pair of them as Harriet clicked on the appropriate symbol and the booking form came into view.

'They fill it in, press 'send', and it comes to us immediately,' she said.

'That's amazing,' said Derek. 'Have you had a lot of them?'

'Mostly bookings by phone so far,' said Harriet.

'And in person,' Rick added.

Derek leaned forward. 'Can I see one of the bookings on the screen?'

'Of course.' Harriet tried to sound confident. They had fallen right into that one. Behind her she felt Derek move slightly and knew exactly how he was feeling. She half expected him to make a swift retreat and leave her to deal with the situation.

She clicked on the appropriate keys. Rick gasped, which he changed hurriedly into a cough. She could hardly believe what she was seeing either.

'A booking for twelve people for a week's tuition,' Rick said in wonder.

'Starting next Saturday,' Harriet said. 'Mixed abilities though.' She tried not to show her disappointment and glanced at Rick, hoping he wouldn't blurt out what she was thinking: that they were bringing their own accommodation — tents — and had booked places already at a campsite somewhere in the area. And so they didn't need anything more from Breaking Waves, only tuition.

'Yep, that's good.'

'And that's the only one I can look at?' said Derek.

Harriet smiled. 'We've only just got the website up and running.' She had seen the email address provided and knew it was Steven's, now at home in Bristol. He had done as he promised and done his best to promote Breaking Waves. It was a good feeling.

After that, Rick got his car out and they drove Derek the short distance to the beach so that he could see for himself where the surfing activities took place. He was interested in the village of Roslarren too, a place he had known from a child on occasional visits to his aunt at Roslarren House. They lingered there quite a while and he pointed out some of the changes that had been made since the old days — some good, some bad.

Dawna, alone in the surf shop, was delighted to meet Rick's father, and he seemed pleased with her input at Breaking Waves.

'A nice, capable girl,' he said in approval. 'It's a pity her shop isn't nearer your place. A better business opportunity, don't you think? All the equipment they'd want to buy immediately on hand and some they wouldn't even think of for themselves.'

Harriet laughed. 'You've got some good ideas, Derek.'

Then it was time to drive to the hotel, a new building on the outskirts of town with a vast car park. Inside was a comfortable reception area where they sat with their drinks waiting for dinner to be served.

It was obvious that in the short time he had been with the other members of his group, Derek had made himself popular. Several of them greeted him by name, full of their day's expedition and wanting to know what Breaking Waves was all about.

'More publicity,' Rick muttered, grinning, in Harriet's ear. 'Too bad it's the wrong sort.'

'Don't be too sure of that,' she said.

'All publicity's good publicity. They might all have grandchildren wanting lessons.'

'Or great grandchildren,' Rick said.

'I heard that,' said Derek, his eyes twinkling at Harriet.

She wondered if she and Rick were being kind in trying to pretend that things were better than they were. But giving Rick's father more cause for alarm wasn't going to help. In a week or two things might be a lot better.

'We don't have an age limit at Breaking Waves,' she said.

Derek smiled. 'I'm glad to hear that, my dear.'

'We should have brought some of our handouts with us.'

'I've got some in the car,' said Rick springing up. 'I won't be a moment.'

It was time now to take their seats in the long, low dining room. Harriet saw that on the walls were original paintings of local scenes, and she recognised one as being that of the Cheesewring. It was outlined against an orange sky and the stones were green. Another painting of the lighthouse at the Lizard was a mass of purples and pinks.

'It makes me seasick just to look at it,' Derek said as he accepted a menu from the waitress who appeared at his side. 'Hello, my dear,' he said, turning to her.

She dimpled at him. 'Good evening, sir.'

Harriet glanced up, taken aback to see Chloë in a short black dress with a miniscule lacy apron tied around her waist.

Rick was back now, exclaiming in pleasure on seeing her again.

'Just on Sundays,' she told him. 'I'm thinking of throwing in my job at the caravan place. Too boring. Are you busy at Breaking Waves?'

'They've just taken a booking for twelve people,' Derek said proudly.

'Twelve?'

'Good, isn't it?'

'I'll say. Then you'll need more help, Rick? There'll be a lot to do for poor

Harriet. I'll be available to help out.'

Rick hesitated and Harriet held her breath.

'He'll let you know,' said Derek firmly. 'I don't know about you two but I'd like to see what's on the menu.'

Chloë seemed suddenly to remember her duties. She whipped out a pen and pad. 'Of course, sir. What can I get for you?' When they had ordered she smiled at Derek. 'I think you must be Rick's father? I saw the likeness at once. You're very alike, aren't you?'

Derek smiled but said nothing. Chloë hesitated for a moment and then whisked away.

Even Rick noticed his father ate very little of his steak and commented on his poor appetite. Harriet tried to deflect him, knowing that it would do no good because Derek must be fully aware of it and didn't need it pointed out.

He seemed too tired afterwards to do little more than go up to his room. They said their goodbyes and left, both subdued.

Dawna called round later, eager to hear his verdict on Breaking Waves. She was pleased to hear they had received a booking while he was with them and how proud he'd been when telling Chloë about it.

'Chloë?'

'It's for twelve,' Rick said. 'Steven's booked them in for Saturday. Chloë wants to come and help since she'll be out of a job when they come. We could let her have somewhere to sleep, couldn't we, Harriet?'

She saw the expression on Dawna's face and was shaken by the raw emotion displayed there. A second later it had gone, hidden behind a smile she suspected was false.

'So you think I can't cope?' Harriet said. 'It's a paid job she's after, and how can we afford that?

'I hadn't thought of that,' Rick admitted.

Harriet smiled. He hadn't thought of a lot of other things either, some right beneath his nose.

# 16

When Dawna left at last, Harriet slipped out of the house and walked down to the beach with the sound of the murmuring sea in her ears. She could smell the soft tang of salt in the air and in the east the moon was rising. A sense of deep peace was settling over land and sea.

And yet this was only an illusion, she thought, as she felt the soft sand beneath her feet. Hidden beneath the peace were the trials that beset everyone at some time or another. But it was good to be here, appreciating it all and hoping that situations could be dealt with and problems solved.

But she didn't know how they could solve the one facing them at Breaking Waves. They had tried so hard to publicise their inclusive surfing holidays. The house was roomy and reasonably comfortable, close to the surfing beach; the menus were worked out well in advance, and the food plentiful; equipment was on hand to be hired at reasonable prices; a qualified instructor would be available . . . the list could go on. The first group had had a good time here, appreciating that they were guinea pigs and glad of the reduced rate they had been offered because of it. But they had had no bookings for the complete package since. Reducing the rates again was simply out of the question or they would soon be running at a loss. But they were running at a loss now.

She sighed, remembering Rick's enthusiasm when he inherited Roslarren House and the idea of running his own surf school had become a possibility. Nothing would deflect him from the plans he was soon making, even though his father had been cautious about the wisdom of it. He feared his son getting into huge debt and losing all he had, including his self-respect, and ending up in the depths of despair, homeless and alone. At first she had thought this an exaggeration, but had soon come to realise that to Derek the fear was a real one and was affecting his health and peace of mind. Because of the past she wanted to reassure him, and so had made the offer to come down here too to help make the business a success.

Now she was beginning to think that her input was of little value and was only adding to Rick's financial problems. She had believed that his idea of offering accommodation as well as tuition was a good one. Had she given up the chance of promotion in a job she loved in vain? But she had done it for Derek. That was the important reason. If Breaking Waves failed, she would have failed too in that respect.

She would also have nowhere to live, and no job. The job prospects here were slim to say the least. So it was likely that she would have to leave Roslarren, a place she loved, and look elsewhere. She thought of Dawna, so friendly and welcoming, and of Jem . . . It was likely she might never see Jem again.

The thought was a painful jolt and for a moment the pain of it was too hard to bear.

Down here on the beach she could feel the gentle breeze from the sea now. Golden light reflected on the water as it surged in and out, leaving soft whirls of white foam on the edge of the sand. For a moment she stood still and breathed deeply. Then she pulled out her mobile phone, scrolled down the list of names and clicked on one of them. 'Jem?'

His voice was low and sent shivers through her as if she hadn't expected to hear it. 'Harriet. So how are you?'

'I haven't thanked you properly for such a good day today.'

'You found it interesting?'

'Oh yes. Yes.'

'I wanted to suggest a meal on the way home but it was not to be. So, how did the visit go?'

'We've got some more bookings. He was pleased with everything. I was glad to see him but he's so weak, Jem. He liked Dawna.'

Jem laughed. 'Most people do. But what's that got to do with it?'

She was babbling. 'I don't know,' she said, confused. 'I'm just glad.'

'Good. I'm sure that'll please her. What are you doing now, Harriet? I was about to phone you.'

'I'm on the beach.'

'Alone?' His tone was sharp.

'There's no one here.'

'Alone then. I'm busy packing. I've only just heard I'm to be in Bristol all week. Various meetings and suchlike.'

So she wouldn't see him. She would be busy too, preparing for the arrivals next Saturday. Even though they weren't using the house, Rick would invite them up there for viewing their progress on-screen, and there was the welcome beach barbecue to prepare for Saturday evening.

'Are you still there, Harriet?'

She shivered. 'It's getting cold. I'll go back now.'

'Look after yourself and I'll see you when I get back.'

And he was gone. The breeze seemed cold now, the moonlight dimmed.

*   *   *

Rick was down on the beach every day, the publicity board in position, enjoying the surf, talking to the lifeguards and hoping for more interest and bookings. But none came.

'There've been no more weeverfish attacks,' he told Harriet when she joined him one afternoon. 'It was bad luck they were around that Sunday. I wish I'd known about it. I'd have collected your surfboard then. I didn't know it was there stored around the back of the lifeguards' hut.'

'How could you if Dawna's note had gone?' said Harriet.

'I could have checked with them. I didn't think of it.'

He looked so downcast that she wanted to reassure him. 'Don't worry about it. We live and learn. I've been drafting a list for Dawna of everything we'll need to have on offer for sale when the group arrive in Saturday. Footwear figures prominently on that.'

'Yep. Good.'

'Come on then. What about my lesson?' He brightened at once.

The surf was good, coming with regularity but not too high. She found herself enjoying the experience, getting a few good runs and not minding when she missed out because there were more coming in behind.

After a while Rick left her to it and she marvelled at the way he swerved in long diagonal sweeps, rejoicing in the extra speed he gained.

On Friday afternoon Dawna joined them, having left her assistant in charge at the shop. Afterwards they walked together up to the house. Dawna had parked her van, packed full of items for sale, in the drive.

Half an hour later, showered and changed, they drank coffee sitting out in the sunshine at the front of the house.

'This is perfect,' Dawna said, finishing her drink and leaning back with her eyes closed.

Harriet smiled to see her. She too felt drowsy and relaxed listening to the murmur of bees and seagulls crying in the distance and with the scent of the honeysuckle wafting across from the boundary wall. 'Someone's coming,' she said.

Dawna's eyes flew open and she sat up straight. 'Oh no, it's that girl. What's she doing here with that great rucksack on her back?' Harriet was wondering that too.

Chloë came jauntily up towards them, smiling. 'Hi there! Where's Rick? I didn't see him in the water.'

'Somewhere down there still,' Harriet replied.

Chloë struggled out of the straps and dropped the rucksack on the ground. 'Phew, that was heavy. All my worldly goods, or as good as. Will he be down there long?'

'We're not his keeper,' Dawna said tartly.

'Any coffee going?'

'I can make you some,' said Harriet, getting up.

'Don't bother. I'll do it. If I'm to be on the staff from now on I'd better make myself at home.'

'But you're not,' said Harriet calmly. 'We came to a decision, Rick and I. We thank you for the offer, but no. There isn't enough work coming in to need more help at the moment. If you'd like to leave your address I'll contact you if we change our minds.'

Chloë laughed. 'I'll wait and see what Rick has to say. You might be surprised.'

'He's coming now,' said Dawna hurriedly. 'I'll leave you to it then, Harriet. I'll bring all the goods I've got for you back later.'

Harriet nodded. 'See you soon.'

Dawna opened the door of her van and got in and then wound down her window to greet Rick. Carrying his surfboard, he came up to her looking as if he'd had the best time of his life. Then he saw Chloë and stopped short.

She went to him, dragging her rucksack. 'You want me here, don't you Rick?' she called out.

Dawna, still in her stationary van, looked on. Harriet, too, although she knew the outcome, was transfixed to see the man in the black wetsuit and the girl in a short white skirt and skimpy top gazing at each other, she with confidence but he looking hounded.

'Sorry, Chloë,' he murmured. 'Hasn't Harriet told you?'

'She wants my address. She'll contact me.' Chloë wrenched one of the zipped side pockets open and pulled out some scraps of paper. 'Here, take this!'

Harriet moved forward to take the piece offered to her and as she did so one of the others fluttered to the ground. The paper was yellow, the writing on it in bold print. Harriet picked it up.

'I've seen that before,' Dawna called down to her.

'You have?' said Rick, surprised.

With a cry Chloë tried to snatch it back, but Harriet held it out of her reach and handed it to Dawna.

Dawna took it in triumph. 'It's the note I attached to your board on the beach to say that Harriet had left because of the weeverfish. Look, Rick, it's the very one. Now you'll believe me!'

'And Chloë had it?'

'So Chloë removed it?' said Harriet.

Rick, in disbelief, stared hard at Chloë, but she didn't wait to brazen it out. She heaved up her rucksack and ran. There was a deep, heartfelt silence.

'Thank goodness she's gone,' said Dawna at last.

'A troublemaker from the beginning,' said Harriet.

But Rick still looked dazed. 'You mean Chloë tore it off deliberately to make you look bad, Dawna?' he said.

'That's about it.'

'She didn't deny it,' Harriet pointed it out.

'Incredible,' Rick muttered. 'I've been a fool.'

'Not for the first time,' Dawna said, laughing. She crumpled the note in her hand and stuffed it in her pocket. 'We're agreed, aren't we, that Chloë did it on purpose to make trouble?'

'I was worried sick,' Rick said.

'She must have known you would be, after all those safety sessions we had,' said Harriet. 'And she knew you'd blame Dawna, and Jem too for carrying me off without a word to anyone. Trouble all round.'

Rick sighed, obviously remembering the outcome of that.

'Don't worry, Rick,' said Dawna. 'It's in the past now and best forgotten, yes? And Jem doesn't bear grudges.'

'But I believed you, Dawna, when you said you'd left the note.'

Harriet smiled. 'So you did. We're well rid of Chloë, Rick. Admit it.'

Suddenly he smiled too. 'Yep, I admit it.' He looked at Dawna as he spoke and she, colouring a little, smiled back.

# 17

By Saturday afternoon Steven's group of twelve had arrived and were ready for their first surfing session. The good weather was holding and the surf was in good order.

After his preliminary talk, Rick gave a pop-up demonstration and then divided the group into two. The obviously proficient ones he took with him into the sea and left the beginners with Harriet for more practice. Then he returned to assess their varying abilities and give help where needed. In the water at last, he stayed with them for a while and then it was Harriet's task to be more involved.

It was hard work for both of them and she was pleased that next day Dawna had promised to be with them. Dawna helped with the barbecue, too, on Saturday evening. As dark fell they sat together talking quietly while someone produced a guitar and others began to dance in the light from the lanterns Rick had placed nearby.

Dawna wanted to know if Rick's father had enjoyed his holiday touring Cornwall. 'I don't know why he doesn't move down here,' she said when she heard he was safely home but hadn't wanted the holiday to end. 'There's plenty of room at Roslarren House.'

Harriet didn't reply. Yes there was plenty of room, but for how long? Dawna sounded confident that it could be arranged quite easily. In fact she seemed confident about everything this evening, as if difficulties could be brushed aside as if she were swatting flies.

⋆ ⋆ ⋆

The week passed slowly, and on Friday afternoon they said goodbye to the members of the group who were enthusiastic about their surfing sessions and promising to come again one day. Harriet suspected that the good weather had had a lot to do with this. Rick had even picked up a couple more bookings for lessons on Tuesday and was well content.

On Sunday morning they were both down on the beach early. The tide was still going out but there was no sunshine today to glint in the patches of water left behind in the hard rutted sand. The lifeguards were not yet on duty but the red and yellow flags marking the area set aside for surfing were in position as Rick set off for the distant sea with his surfboard under one arm. Harriet watched him go, his figure getting smaller and smaller, until he reached the sea and plunged into it with obvious pleasure. She had decided to stay by their noticeboard for a while, enjoying the fresh salty air on her face and the feeling of vast emptiness of sand sea and sky. Even from this distance she could see a few other surfers in the water. They looked like lithe seals in their black wetsuits and for a moment she pretended they were.

After a while she picked up her surfboard, still one of the smaller ones, and joined Rick in the water. It was becoming busy now and she soon lost sight of him. It was some time before she noticed that the horizon was invisible behind a mass of dark clouds that looked as if they would soon have covered the whole sky. The weather was on the turn.

There were more surfers in the water than there had been before. Or had she been so engrossed with getting some good runs she hadn't noticed? She glanced at the shore, so much nearer now. One more wave and she would go.

As she waited for it she felt drops of rain on her face. Here it was . . . now! She had timed it perfectly and, exhilarated, she headed in, determined to enjoy her last wave of the day.

Suddenly, with a whoosh, a black figure cut across her path and the next moment she was floundering in the water. Her board shot into the air and came down again, pulled back by the leash.

The next thing she knew she was lying flat on the beach, the lowering sky blotted out by the figure of a lifeguard bending over her.

★ ★ ★

'I saw that,' said Rick's indignant voice. 'I saw it happen. It was no accident. She came at Harriet deliberately, right across her bows.'

'She?' said the lifeguard, sitting back on his heels.

'Someone who wants to get her own back on Breaking Waves.'

A crowd had gathered, mainly surfers. Someone in shorts and a fleecy jacket with his rain-wet hair plastered to his head took a photo. '*Cornwall Echo*,' he said in explanation. 'Breaking Waves?'

Rick, still incensed, frowned. He had said too much. But it was too late, much too late to take anything back from something that was likely to prove a good story.

Through a hazy mist Harriet was aware of questions and non-committal answers that fooled nobody. She tried to sit up. 'My head!'

'Stay still. The paramedics are on their way.'

'But I'm all right.'

Someone had untied the leash on her surfboard. Now she was lifted onto it and with the help of another of the lifeguards carried up on it to their hut. There Rick stayed by her side until she had been checked and pronounced fit enough to go home if someone could provide a lift.

There was no problem with that and five minutes later she was at Roslarren House, thankful to be away from the publicity she found so irksome.

'The door's unlocked,' said Rick in surprise. He pushed it open and then stopped in dismay.

Horrified, Harriet saw the posters torn from the wall, the contents of the cupboard at the far end of the hall tipped out and scattered. They went in, stepping over the debris and pushing open doors to gaze in disbelief at the mess they found in the dining room in particular. The leads to the television set had been cut but it was otherwise untouched. The laptop had gone and so had the box of memory sticks Harriet had left on the table, meaning to put them away later. In the kitchen the important papers she kept in one of the drawers had been emptied out and torn to shreds to fall like giant snowflakes on the floor.

With a cry of rage Rick rushed out to check the surfboards, wetsuits and other gear kept in one of the outside rooms. Harriet sank down at the table and sat with her head in her hands, defeated. Someone wished them ill. Someone hated them so much that she would do this horrible thing. Or arrange someone else to do it for her.

Rick was back now, flushed and determined. She raised her head, afraid to ask after more damage.

'Nothing touched out there,' he said. 'I'll phone the police.'

The kitchen phone was untouched, like the one in the dining room. Rick spoke rapidly, his voice deeper than usual as he explained what had happened.

Harriet looked at him. 'We've lost everything.'

'I'll check upstairs.'

She didn't want to move, to see anything more for herself. It was enough to listen to Rick's footsteps on the bare boards of the rooms above, the crash of doors and at last more thumps on the stairs.

'Beds stripped, a mess everywhere,' he said shortly.

'Don't touch anything,' said Harriet. But she didn't care if he did. She didn't care about anything. A dreadful lethargy had taken over and all she could do was sit here and never want to move again.

Rick strode backwards and forwards, unable to sit still, deciding to make a list of missing objects and looking round in vain for something to write on. 'The laptop's gone,' he said. 'That's all?'

'Your smartphone?'

He looked at her as if he had never heard of such a thing. 'My mobile's in my bag.'

'Or *was*.' She didn't really care but got up to look. She found the bag and its contents safely at the bottom of her cupboard in her room where she had left it. Rick's smartphone was the only other thing missing as far as they could determine.

Time passed. The police came. Afterwards Rick phoned Dawna and she came at once, as horrified to see the damage as they had been. 'And we know who's responsible,' she said. 'You told the police?' Neither answered and she looked from one to the other in growing disbelief.

'We've lost all our records,' Harriet said hopelessly.

'All of them?'

'Even the memory sticks. Someone hates Breaking Waves and wants us to close down.'

'Not Jem,' said Dawna with conviction.

The idea was crazy, yet Harriet couldn't help dwelling on it for just an instant.

'Of course it wasn't Jem,' said Rick.

'So his good name is cleared even before I give him an alibi?'

He looked astonished. 'What sort of conversation is this?'

Dawna shrugged. 'It's the shock talking.'

Harriet feared that it was. Rick hadn't mentioned Chloë, and yet he must have been wondering. The police knew that Chloë was annoyed with them, that was all.

\*   \*   \*

Later that evening the press arrived. They recognised the journalist from the *Cornish Echo* but not the sunburned young man with a shock of auburn hair who took up a position by the gate.

The ringing of the doorbell made

them all jump. 'I'll go,' said Harriet.'

'Don't tell them anything,' said Rick, sounding desperate.

Dawna was scornful. 'As if she would. Have a bit of sense, Rick.'

It wasn't as hard as Harriet had thought. For one thing, she had the backing of Dawna and Rick, who followed her along the passage and stood stolidly behind her as she opened the door just a short way. She ignored the questions that were shot at her.

'A bit of a clean-up job and then business as usual,' she said clearly and, to her own ears, much too loudly. She hoped they hadn't picked up on the hint of rising panic in her voice it was impossible to control. She stretched her mouth in a smile and as she saw a camera raised, ducked back inside and slammed the door. Rick turned the key in the lock.

'Well done,' Dawna breathed as Rick pulled the bolts across, top and bottom.

'The blinds should have been closed downstairs,' said Rick. 'I'll see to it.'

No one said that it was probably too late. They returned to the kitchen, which had come off best as the intruders rampaged through the rest of the house. Harriet and Dawna between them replaced the contents of two of the drawers in the unit that had been left hanging open.

'You should go home, Dawna,' said Rick when that was done.

She hesitated. 'I suppose so.'

'But she'll be mobbed,' said Harriet.

'Not if she goes the back way.'

Dawna nodded. 'Good thinking. I'll collect the van tomorrow.'

'Phone as soon as you get in,' Harriet urged.

Dawna gave a gurgling laugh. 'I'm not likely to be attacked, or hounded even. But, yes, I'll do that.'

Harriet wouldn't normally have thought so, but now she was beginning to believe that anything might happen. She sat down hurriedly again as Rick locked the back door behind Dawna.

# 18

The heavy rain during the night must have discouraged the two watchers outside because there was no sign of them when Harriet peered out of her window next morning, taking care not to be seen. But by breakfast time they were back, joined by three others.

'It's no good,' said Rick, pushing his chair back and standing up.

'What are you going to do?' Harriet slotted some bread in the toaster. Neither of them was hungry, but they had to eat.

'Tell them to clear off.'

'Wait, Rick. Please. If we do nothing they'll get tired of hanging around and go away. Breaking Waves will be old news by tomorrow.'

'You think?' He flopped down in his chair again and looked on gloomily as Harriet spread bread with marmalade.

Then he took a piece of toast for himself and ate it just as it was.

The wind was getting up now and after a while there was the patter of rain on the window, invisible behind the closed blind.

The phone rang and Harriet got up to answer it. The two people booked in for surfing lessons next day had decided to cancel. She put down the receiver and for a moment stood looking down at it. She felt Rick staring at her and glanced up to see the expression of concern on his face.

'A cancellation?'

She shrugged. 'I'm afraid so. The one for tomorrow, the only one. It's not good.' In silence she cleared the table and started on the washing up.

The phone rang again. 'Your turn,' she said. With her back to him she listened to his side of the conversation, but it wasn't making much sense. 'What was all that about?' she said as he finished the call.

'Thunderstorms are forecast for the

end of the week.'

She gazed at him in astonishment. 'And who rang to tell you that?'

'Jem Williams, if you must know.'

'Jem?'

'I knew he'd been talking to Dawna, but she wouldn't tell me what about. But then he had a word with me, too, last week when I saw him over at his place.'

'You didn't tell me.'

'His house has been on the market for a while but he's got a good offer on it now. He knows the situation here is even more serious than it was and wants to act straight away.'

She was horrified. 'You mean you'd sell out to him?'

'Not sell necessarily.'

'Then what?' She felt her lips tremble.

'Think of the state of this place — the records all gone, things stolen. How can we make a go of it now?'

'We can try. We can build it up again.'

'And lose loads of money while we're doing it?'

Harriet found it hard to speak. She tried to swallow the lump in her throat and in doing so brought tears to her eyes. She turned away so that Rick shouldn't see. What would his dad have to say about this? Would he accept Rick's sudden decision knowing that financially his son wouldn't be losing on the deal? Derek Seton was a realist. She had considered herself one, too, until now.

'But having your own surf school meant so much to you, Rick,' she said. 'And you love the house.'

It was too much. All her work for nothing ... except that Jem would obviously gain something close to his heart, a place in Roslarren where he wanted to be. But she had to think of Rick. 'You can finish clearing up down here,' she said. 'I've got things to do upstairs.'

She was reminded of Chloë flouncing off when things didn't suit her. Rick had given the impression he didn't know what he wanted now, and Jem would be quick to take advantage. She had assured Derek that she would have his son's interests at heart and she must keep that promise.

She moved from room to room, pulling up blinds and letting in gloomy daylight. It was the matter of moments to get the mattresses back on the beds. Most of them hadn't been made up with bedding and on these she replaced the bedspreads she kept in place to make the rooms look lived in. The sheets, pillow cases and duvet covers on the others she removed. Someone had touched them as they yanked at the beds, someone wishing ill to Breaking Waves. She wanted all memories of that washed away.

In the airing cupboard she found clean linen, and once the beds were made up the rooms looked much as normal. She checked the bathrooms and found nothing untoward there. So far so good. The accommodation upstairs was as it should be, waiting for someone to occupy it.

Every now and again she heard the phone ring, and once banging on the back door, and then silence again. But it all seemed removed from her, marooned as she was up here in a house she couldn't leave. She moved across to her bedroom window and gazed out at the damp world. The sea was a sheet of grey with occasional bursts of white foam, but there were no good waves rolling in today. And where were the seagulls' squawks and cries? It was a silent world out there where nothing moved.

With relief she was aware the journalists had left them now. Rick had noticed too, because he appeared on the drive wearing his wetsuit and with his surfboard under one arm. She watched him go slowly down to the beach. He must surely know that he would be the only one down there. No good surf today, and no hope of any from what she could see.

She had time now to think, to go over and over in her mind all that had happened since she came down here to Roslarren full of hope and commitment. She thought of Jem on the beach after that first barbecue, with his dark head thrown back and the light of discovery on his face as he saw in those cliffs things that others didn't see. That was how he was: imaginative and clear-sighted, knowing what he wanted and going for it.

Rick, though, was different. Although he knew what he wanted too, or thought he did, he didn't always go about getting it in the most direct way. He needed someone like Dawna to laugh her way out of problems and jolly him along. Maybe he would work in her surf shop and find some satisfaction in that. But no, not Rick. The thought pained her.

She couldn't see him now because the lifeguards' hut was in the way. She hoped they were there and he could linger and chat. It was what he needed, someone else to talk to and in a different environment than being imprisoned in Roslarren House.

Dawna phoned later to invite them both to an evening meal at her flat. 'I'll close early and that will give me plenty of time to prepare a feast for the two of you.'

'Business is slack?'

'Fallen right away. But it'll pick up as soon as the sun shines.'

'If that ever happens.'

Dawna's throaty laugh echoed in Harriet's head and she smiled too.

By the time Rick returned for lunch Harriet had cleaned up the mess in the hall and washed the floor. He came in the back way, leaving his board outside.

Harriet heard voices and then saw with a swift thud of her heart that Jem was with him. More business talk, involving her this time?

'I can't stop,' Jem said, seeing her anxious expression. 'Dawna wanted me to join you this evening but I can't make it. How do you feel about coming out with me for the day tomorrow, Harriet, to get you away from all this for a short time?'

'But I have to . . . '

'No problem,' said Rick.

Jem looked at her closely. 'You need time to get things into perspective away from here. You need space, Harriet, and there's plenty of that on Bodmin Moor.'

She couldn't argue with that.

'I thought a visit to the Cheesewring. What do you say to that?'

'Well, yes . . . ' The Cheesewring? Full circle then, except that she hadn't reached the Cheesewring.

'The Hurlers too,' he said. 'Did you get there?'

She shook her head. 'I'm a failure all round.'

His smile was enigmatic. 'Be ready at nine.'

'And if it rains?'

'No matter.'

'And those thunderstorms?'

'Are you making difficulties?'

'There are plenty of those,' she said.

'Then a few more will make no difference.'

It was clear he wasn't going to be deflected, and she was too tired to argue. 'I'll be ready,' she said.

He nodded, gave an indication of farewell to Rick and was off, striding down the drive as if he already owned it.

# 19

'We'll go to Trelevy Quoit first,' said Jem. 'It's on the way and I'd like you to see it. Is that all right with you?'

Harriet fastened her safety belt and turned to smile at him. She was glad to be warm and dry inside his Land Rover instead of out there with her head down against the drizzling rain.

'Fine,' she said as they set off. 'Trelevy Quoit, you said? Is that one of those constructions of huge stones with a huge slanting sheet of rock balanced on top? I've seen pictures of them.' They were leaving Roslarren now, heading for the Bodmin road with the surroundings misted with rain.

'Cornwall's full of them,' Jem said. 'But this one has a special meaning for me. My grandfather's farm wasn't far away. I went there a lot. It had a great deal to do with my interest in archaeology.'

'Is it very old?'

'3,500 B.C. Neolithic or early Bronze Age, at the time of the first farmers on the moor.'

She was silenced, trying to take in the enormity of time between then and now and how different life would have been for those people.

They joined the dual carriageway and sped along with the windscreen wipers working overtime. She wondered where the streams of traffic on the other side were going so purposefully on this dismal day. Then she thought of their arrival at Trelevy Quoit and being unable to see anything through the mist and rain. At her side Jem seemed unperturbed.

'It'll ease off soon,' he said.

The countryside was becoming bleaker now that the cloud was lower, and she began to feel a sense of loss because they were hastening away from Roslarren and the brightness and the activity there. But it would be raining there, too, and the sky would be as lowering and leaden-grey. But it felt as if an elastic thread was trying to draw her back to a life that felt right for her. She was afraid it would get so tight it would snap.

By the time they turned off the A30 to join the Liskeard road the rain had become a thin drizzle. They drove past trees, their new foliage dripping and dim in the misty light. Then they were into open moorland as they turned off this road onto a minor one. They rattled over a cattle grid.

'Not far now,' he said.

Eventually they reached the village of Darite and Jem drove slowly down a right-hand turning that was so narrow between high banks that Harriet wondered they could get through. Here the grass, close up, looked luxurious and was dotted with bluebells and delicate white stitchwort. She smiled, imagining she could smell the sweet bluebell scent through the glass of her window.

'And you've driven here before?' she said.

'Once or twice.' Jem's tongue protruded a little between his lips in concentration.

And then they were there. He turned deftly into the small area for parking. They got out.

Higher up on the other side of the lane just before a group of dwellings was a kissing gate. As she went through, Harriet was taken by surprise at the height of the upended stones that centuries ago someone had built up with a massive capstone as a slanting roof. She could see that Jem was as moved as she was even though he knew it well.

'So was it used as a burial chamber?' she said.

'It's likely it held the bones of the dead. It would never have been completely covered, just the earth and stone round the bottom. They think it had other uses too: marking a community territory, for example, and as a gathering place for the ceremonial life of the community.'

'That makes sense,' she said. She walked over the wet grass to the other side and saw that one of the massive flat stones had fallen inwards. She noticed a hole near the top, too, and turned to Jem to ask what it had been for.

'I'll tell you about that later,' he said. He looked at his watch. 'Seen enough now?'

She nodded.

'There's plenty more to see. At least it's stopped raining now.'

They drove back the way they had come down the narrow lane and then took another road that was just as narrow but on open moorland. She saw ponies in the distance, brown and white, and the black cattle with wide bands of white she had seen on her first visit.

'Belted Galloway cattle,' Jem said when she remarked on them.

'I feel sorry for them out in weather like this,' she said.

He laughed. 'The livestock play a big part in preserving the habitat. They stop it becoming overgrown with bracken and scrub.'

'That's good of them.'

'And that's Caradon Hill on our right,'

he said. 'See the television masts?'

He ignored the place where she had parked her car on her way down to Roslarren and drove through the village of Minions to park in the larger space set aside for the purpose.

The wind almost wrenched the door out of Harriet's hand as she got out. Jem looked anxiously at the sky. 'Right. The Cheesewring. Ready to go?'

She zipped her jacket up as high as she could. 'I'm ready.'

A short distance away she saw, stark against the grey sky, a ruined engine house. Avoiding it, they set off up the track side by side. She had seen pictures of the Cheesewring and so she knew what to expect, but she wasn't at all sure she wanted to see it in real life now with the wind biting her face and her eyes watering. The ground was rutted and it seemed to be going on forever.

Jem turned to her. 'All right?' The wind took the words out of his mouth but she knew what they were. She nodded.

Suddenly there was a gust, stronger

than before, and a single clap of thunder. Then the rain came again, slanting in their faces so fiercely that they stopped for a moment, uncertain what to do.

'We'll have to go back,' Jem said sharply. 'Come on, Harriet — run.' He took hold of her hand and they left the track and ran, slipping and sliding over the rough ground. She was breathless by the time they arrived at the engine house that she now saw had a flight of wooden steps leading to a solid door. Moments later they were inside, water dripping from their clothes and laughing at the state they were in.

'Sorry about that,' said Jem. 'You're a great girl, Harriet.'

She had been cold an instant ago. Now the warmth from his words made her face glow. Jem pulled off his jacket and she did too. They left them on a bench by the door.

Harriet pushed her streaming hair out of her eyes. 'So what's this place now?'

'It's a heritage centre,' he said. 'Once an engine house for a tin mine, long since disused.'

'Well yes, I can see that now,' she said, looking around at the exhibition showing the history of the moor and much else besides. But for the moment she was too exhausted to do anything more than sink down on one of the chairs to regain her breath.

'The fierceness of that took me by surprise,' Jem said.

'And you knowing Bodmin Moor like the back of your hand!'

He grinned. 'You're not mad at me?'

She looked up at him, her heart full as he stood in front of her, gazing at her with his head held a little to one side. She wanted to tell him then how much he meant to her, but instead she stood up to examine some of the charts on the wall. He had brought her out today to explain his reasons for wanting to purchase Roslarren House and she already knew those well enough. Rick, it seemed, was on the verge of accepting

Jem's offer. It was Rick's decision she couldn't understand. But why should it be Jem who felt the need to explain it to her?

On one of the charts was the information that Bodmin Moor had been worked by man for the past six thousand years that Jem had already told her. She still found it hard to take in. She read it again in an effort to do so. She could certainly understand Jem's deep interest in these far-away times. She wanted to know more about the traces those early people had left behind them. That and the geology of the area which must have played a huge part in their lives.

'So you want to combine the study and the conservation of our geological heritage with the prehistoric remains?' she said. 'Have I got that right?'

He smiled. 'More or less. Just as I also want to combine my interests with Rick's.'

'How do you mean?'

'How would you feel if Rick and I

combined our business interests? It's the obvious solution for all our problems, for me to have a half share of Roslarren House by either purchase or lease. We could then work in conjunction with each other. And you are the link, Harriet. An important link.'

'And that's why you brought me out today?'

A strange expression flitted across his face. 'I had something more important in mind, but that too. It means a lot to me to know your opinion on our plans before we go ahead.'

'Tell me.'

'During the summer months Rick will hold surfing courses with or without accommodation. In the winter I will do the same with my geoconservation groups.'

'And in spring and autumn?'

'By arrangement, as it will be at the other times, too, depending on bookings. The house is big enough to cope with it all. That way the facilities will have continual use and we share expenses. Dawna, too, will give up the lease of her shop and have a retail outlet at Roslarren House instead. I've had some serious talks with her about that.'

'And me?'

'You'll be in general charge of the running of the place.'

'You've thought it all through very carefully.'

'It was Erica who gave me the germ of the idea on the geological walk at Trebarwith Strand.'

Harriet smiled. 'So she'll get her sandy beach while her husband is being taken care of by you?'

'That's about it. There may be other couples who have separate interests, too, and can be accommodated.'

Harriet laughed. 'You're even cleverer than I thought you were.'

'But not in accurate weather forecasting.'

'In other things that matter.'

'I could tell you a lot about the Cheesewring now because it doesn't look as if we'll get there this time. But this isn't the right moment. I'm assuming you think the plan is a good one?'

'It could be.'

'It could mean the likely end of the financial worries for Breaking Waves and give me the base I need in the Roslarren area as well.'

'There's one thing you haven't mentioned. Where will we all live?'

'I was coming to that.'

'And?'

'The house has so much potential. It wouldn't be difficult to convert part of it to make two self-contained units, and we could expand. In fact that would be a good idea if Rick's father feels he'd like to make his home down here, too.'

Harriet gazed at him, speechless.

'There'll be a lot to organise, of course,' he went on. 'I've a feeling that Rick and Dawna have a good thing going for them. In fact I know they have. Do you think we could have, too?'

Suddenly she was filled with a sense of deep joy. Just now she had been walking with Jem with the wind stirring her hair and making her eyes smart. And then the rain had come, soaking them in minutes as they ran to the safety of this building hand in hand. But now it seemed as if golden light shone all round them and the world was beautiful.

'Jem?' she whispered.

And then she was in his arms, his lips on hers.

They broke away and she saw that a shaft of sudden sunshine shone through the window, reflecting on the shiny surface of the glass case opposite.

'A good omen, my dearest Harriet,' he murmured. 'And look, the clouds are clearing.'

They stood together at the window and looked out at the brown and boggy landscape that now seemed magical to her because of the man at her side. In the distance she saw the three rings of standing stones she assumed were the Hurlers.

'You know the story?' he said. 'Someone organised a ball game of hurling on the Sabbath and this was the punishment. The players were all turned to stone and have been there ever since.' He laughed at her expression. 'People told their children that to make sure they behaved themselves on Sundays. A myth, of course. A bit like telling them that babies are found under gooseberry bushes.'

'Babies?'

'We can bring our children here.'

'And grandchildren.'

He smiled so sweetly that her heart melted with longing. This was no myth. This was real and true and lasting. She thought suddenly of Trelevy Quoit standing there for thousands of years. 'What was that hole I saw in the stone near the top?' she said.

He knew at once what she meant. 'Ah! The Merriment Hole. There's a tradition there, too, but I didn't have pen or paper on me.'

'You didn't?'

'If I had, I could have written an important question on it. Pushed through that hole, it would have stood a good chance of coming true.'

She giggled. 'Can I guess what it was?'

'I think you know that, don't you, my love?'

But before she could say anything she was in his arms again, his lips pressing down hard on hers so that she had no doubt at all what it might have been.

## THE END

We do hope that you have enjoyed reading this large print book.

Did you know that all of our titles are available for purchase?

We publish a wide range of high quality large print books including:
**Romances, Mysteries, Classics**
**General Fiction**
**Non Fiction and Westerns**

Special interest titles available in large print are:
**The Little Oxford Dictionary**
**Music Book, Song Book**
**Hymn Book, Service Book**

Also available from us courtesy of Oxford University Press:
**Young Readers' Dictionary**
**(large print edition)**
**Young Readers' Thesaurus**
**(large print edition)**

For further information or a free brochure, please contact us at:
**Ulverscroft Large Print Books Ltd.,**
**The Green, Bradgate Road, Anstey,**
**Leicester, LE7 7FU, England.**
**Tel:** (00 44) 0116 236 4325
**Fax:** (00 44) 0116 234 0205

*Other titles in the*
*Linford Romance Library:*

## MISTRESS ANGEL

## Lindsay Townsend

London, 1357. Once a child bride, married off to halt a blood feud between rich and ambitious families, Isabella is now a tormented young widow. When her beloved son Matthew is torn away from her care, spirited somewhere into the country by her malicious in-laws, Isabella is desperate. To save her son she will do anything, risk anything. Even if it means she must lose the love of her life, the handsome armorer Stephen Fletcher . . .

# THE LOOK OF LOVE

## Marilyn Fountain

What happens when your impetuous step-sister goes on holiday to Italy engaged to one man, and then comes home with another? And not only that, but neither fiancé is aware of the other's existence! Before she knows it, Beth Tilney has promised to keep Lauren's double love life a secret — for now. And that's far from easy, especially when the Italian fiancé's cousin and best man, the intriguing and attractive Roberto Di Ferraio, arrives to keep an eye on things, and proves to be a big distraction . . .

# MRS. CATT'S CURIOSITIES

## Monica Brent

She sells anything and everything
— but more than that, she sells
hope . . . Ken Weaver has just about
hit rock bottom when he comes
across Mrs. Cart's Curiosities. And
before he knows it, he is leaving the
store with a very special purchase
. . . But can an old medal really heal
a family that has been torn apart?
Meanwhile, Jay Randall has spent
the better part of a year nursing a
broken heart. But thanks to Mrs.
Catt and a faded old photograph, he
meets a beautiful girl named Cece,
and learns to love again.

# JUNGLE FEVER

## Carol MacLean

Eager to climb out from under the shadow of her famous mother, Eva manages to secure a place on a scientific expedition to the Amazon, determined to prove her own worth. But her steamy surroundings quickly build up heat of a different nature, as she finds herself increasingly attracted to the eminently desirable Dan. Then two surprise additions to the expedition turn everything upside-down. Will jealousies, family strife, and the deadly dangers of the tropics get in the way of Eva and Dan's future happiness?

OKANAGAN REGIONAL LIBRARY

3 3132 03684 8630